Betrayal

ASHLEY McCARTHY

AMP

Betrayal – Winners and Losers Book 1

Copyright © Ashley McCarthy, 2022

ISBN: 2nd Print edition – 978-1-7395046-1-8
          Digital edition – 978-1-8384121-5-9

Published by:

AMP

ASHLEY McCARTHY
PUBLISHING

www.ashley-mccarthy.com

Typesetting and Production: Catherine Williams, Chapter One Book Production
Cover Design: Andrew Newman Design

Printed in the United Kingdom

Dedication

Dedicated to myself.
Because I keep pulling this off!

Prologue

Moonlight glinted on the ocean as the yacht drifted to a slow halt, bobbing gently on the calm, midnight waters. Kent stumbled as he made his way to the seating area. The other guys were sleeping, passed out after their drug-fuelled evening on the mainland.

It's been a good night, Kent reflected as he grabbed an open bottle of gin from the floor. Swigging on the dregs, he sat down with a thud on the Italian leather bench and leaned back, closing his eyes. He pulled a hand down his stubbled cheek and recalled the evening's indulgence, allowing the memory of the gentleman's club to wash over him. The smell of sweat and euphoria filled his nostrils as he thought of the sea of heaving bodies in Coco, the nightclub along the shore of Cannes.

And then out on to the open water.

The boat bobbed rhythmically through the night hours. While waves gently lapped at the hull, the darkness slowly faded. The first rays of sun bled over the peaked water, gradually edging towards the boat and pulling the souls on board into wakefulness. They began to stir.

Kent blinked hard as he looked around. 'Where's George?' he asked, his voice hoarse from the gin.

Joseph stretched then stood up. After looking around in brief confusion, he moved to the side of the yacht. 'There's someone in the water!' he yelled in a panic as he leaned over the rail.

Kent hastened to the side of the yacht. He watched the body floating face down in the waves, bobbing with the same cadence as the boat, briefly closing his eyes in realisation. Too late.

He stripped his blazer, kicked off his shoes, and with the elegance of an Olympic diver, plunged in. The cold water hit him with a sobering slap. There was a splash next to him as Joseph pitched himself alongside. They swam to the body, heaving it over to confirm its identity, then between them pulled it back to the yacht, lifting it as best they could so the other men could drag George's body aboard.

Kent paused in the water for a moment, his eyes locked on Joseph. The moment passed in slow motion, neither wanting to face the scene awaiting them above. Eventually, they hoisted themselves on deck. The body had already begun to whiten, its lifeless eyes fixed skyward. Even so, Joseph dropped to his knees and pushed frantically on the water-logged chest. His efforts continued for some time.

'It's too late,' said David.

Kent picked up the boat's radio and called the coastguard.

George had gone.

'À l'aide … à l'aide … nous avons un blessé à bord … nous avons besoin de secours,' he barked.

Joseph sat back, shaking his head. David opened his mouth as if to say something, but no sound emerged. They stared helplessly down at George's body.

Joseph turned his anguished eyes to Kent. 'His family …' he moaned.

Kent nodded, his mouth set into a grim line. His business partner and long-time friend was gone.

Someone had to tell Inés.

Chapter One

'Are we nearly there yet?' came Erin's voice from some-where above, in a childish tone that belied her sixteen years. Inés rolled her eyes. Erin's gazelle-like legs came over the back of the cab seats and she settled down to keep her mum company for the last part of the journey. The early morning beamed through the window and bathed them in its light, picking out the natural highlights in Erin's auburn hair. Inés gazed at her daughter, taken aback as she so often was these days by how fast her eldest daughter was growing up.

'Mum!' Erin cried. Inés snapped her eyes back to the road. They were heading straight towards a huge fallen oak tree on the verge up ahead. The narrow track swung sharply to the right and Inés jerked at the steering wheel. The huge artic lorry was pulled out of its potentially dev-astating trajectory just in time. They missed mounting the verge and the tree by inches, not without tipping some breakables in the kitchenette, Inés cringed at the smash-ing sound. The winding roads that led to many British showgrounds were treacherous and, in most cases, not up to the job of accommodating lorries. Inés breathed a sigh of relief as the road started to widen ahead.

'Some driving, huh?' she joked to lighten the moment, now keeping her eyes fixed ahead.

Erin snorted with teenage disapproval. 'Apart from the nearly killing us, mum, it was brilliant,' she muttered. Inés checked the video feed attached to the dashboard. On-screen the ponies were munching their hay happily in the back of the lorry, unaware of the trouble they had narrowly avoided.

Inés smiled again. She reflected on how much Erin was starting to sound and look like her father. Feeling a bittersweet wave of nostalgia, Inés couldn't believe it had been four years since George had been taken from her on that damn boys' boating holiday. Although Inés had kept the family and her career together as best she could since then, it hadn't been easy, especially with five children. Taking the girls to their activities was a welcome distraction from the pressure of work and grieving. She had to run their home like a boot camp to keep everyone fed, clothed, punctual and, above all, happy. Accompanying the children like this gave her the chance to enjoy them. Inés was happiest here, indulging them. It also became her way of masking the guilt she harboured for the loss of their father.

Inés was often distracted by her job. It was a lot of pressure and she'd always been the sort of woman who burned the candle at both ends. This worsened after George had gone; Inés made sure she never had a spare second to stop and think of the hole he'd left. Wrong decisions at work cost their investors money, and as Chief Financial Officer at Clydfell Capital Management in London, the buck stopped with her.

'To answer your original question,' Inés said, 'We *are* nearly there, so I hope you're prepared and ready for battle.' She tried to inject as much motivation into her voice as she could after the five o'clock start. Inés could have asked one of their grooms to take Erin to the show, so she could get on with work, but had decided against it. Inés' phone had been planted against her ear for most of the journey while Erin slept in the Luton above the cab, cosy with pillows, blankets and a big faux fur rug. Her daughter's success was too important to miss. Erin was never at her best when she hadn't had enough sleep. *What teenager was?* Inés thought.

'Yeah,' Erin mumbled as they eventually pulled into the lorry park.

Inés gave a spirited pat atop her daughter's leg. 'Come on. Glory awaits,' she said lightly.

Erin hopped out of the lorry, then stretched out her long limbs, looking around with a yawn. The mornings were still chilly as winter ebbed into the warmth of spring. She pulled a baseball cap over a tangle of waist-length hair and started with the usual routine of unloading equipment and organising her number bib that she'd wear while competing that day. Inés could see her daughter flapping about where missing pieces of equipment were and the all-too-common look of worry beginning to take hold on Erin's face.

A sea of horse lorries and trailers was neatly lined up

in a large flat field that was used as a makeshift car park on competition days. They were directed by volunteer stewards wearing hi-vis tabards who didn't seem entirely sure what they were supposed to be doing, but sported big smiles, anyway. Parking in fields in the UK was never a good idea, but no matter how many times heavy vehicles got stuck in the sludge, show organisers seemed completely surprised by the chaos. Shows during the months of bad weather usually brought out armies of tractors, desperately pulling beached lorries over to solid tarmac so their wheels could get some purchase. Even so, the damage left after competitions never spurred them into spending money on creating better parking facilities.

As the morning wore on, the crowds grew and competitors busied themselves scrubbing stains off their ponies' legs or pulling perfectly polished boots over cream-coloured breeches and knee-length socks. There was always a buzz of activity early morning at equestrian shows; parents asking other competitors if they could borrow a forgotten piece of equipment, or dawdling children chatting amongst themselves and being told by harried parents that they must mount their ponies and warm up before being called into the arena.

As they were unloading the ponies, Inés spotted the de Bohun's lorry. Quickly, she flapped her hand at Erin, signalling to keep a low profile, but instead managed to alert Elizabeth de Bohun to her presence. Inés immediately turned the gesture into a friendly wave and busied herself with nothing in particular in the hope she and Erin would be left alone. The de Bohuns continued setting up their infamous drinks station next to their luxurious lorry. This social ritual was as important to them as the competition.

It wasn't that Inés disliked the de Bohuns exactly, in fact they could be good fun in the right circumstances, but their pomposity was sometimes too much for her liking. This was 'rich' coming from Inés. Her friends teased her whenever she brought up the de Bohuns, pointing out she was prone to being a snob herself at times. The de Bohuns lived in Stathum Manor, not far from Inés and the girls, in what could only be described as a vast and spectacular Queen Anne mansion, and rarely wasted an opportunity to inform people that they went by the titles of Earl and Countess. 'Just to keep people properly informed, of course,' Lady Elizabeth would insist, as if it were a hardship she must endure. Their son, Benjamin, who was the same age as Erin and also competing today, was the most spoiled and conceited child Inés had ever met. She occasionally heard some of the riders on the circuit exclaim their annoyance to each other because he'd stuck out a foot and tripped them over, or told them the competition would be too difficult for them moments before they'd enter the ring. It certainly seemed to Inés that this was more than bullying. He was purposefully trying to alter the playing field in his favour; he hated losing. When he was younger, Inés had seen him throwing tantrums – blaming his ponies for not coming first. On one of these occasions, he'd launched a whip in frustration, avoiding Inés' head by a hair's breadth. She was thankful her girls didn't like him. One less teenage boy to worry about. *He'll be serious trouble one day,* she thought.

Inés pushed the dread of small talk with the de Bohuns aside. Erin getting placed and securing her spot at the coming British qualifiers in Spain was the only thing that mattered *and* the reason they'd driven to Warwickshire from their home in the Surrey Hills. Erin was jumping three of her ponies today but was hoping to qualify just one, her pride and joy, Million Dollar Baby. If she could get on the British team with anyone, it would be with him. They made it to the final 'jump-off' round during the qualifiers last weekend, but they were knocked out of the qualifying spots by a few fractions of a second; Erin was heartbroken. Making it over those big fences had to be done with speed, skill and accuracy. That weekend the fences had been built up to maximum height for Erin's age group, and were intimidating to both pony and rider. 'Baby' had attacked every fence with bravery, but the problem wasn't courage, it was speed. Baby trusted Erin and he always tried his best for her, no matter what she asked or how hard and technical the course of jumps was. To win, a rider not only had to clear all the fences in the first round, but then clear a second course of fewer, taller fences, in the fastest time.

Where Erin had only recognised her performance last weekend as a failure, Inés saw it for what it was; self-doubt. Erin needed to relax and focus out there. Inés knew her daughter was good enough; she'd proved it time and time again over the years. But something was different now, something was affecting her daughter in a way it never had before. The margins were narrow at the top level of showjumping. You had to give the classes your all every day to succeed. And that bit of air between winner or loser was only in a competitor's psyche.

Inés reassured her eldest daughter that it happened to everyone once in a while and managed to hide her doubt when they discussed strategy. This was happening too often and couldn't be pinned on an 'off day'. She admired Erin's determination, though she couldn't help but worry that unless something changed, Erin's neurosis would keep holding her back. Inés thought of her second daughter, Caoimhe. If only she could bottle *her* laid-back attitude and give it to Erin. Caoimhe was thirteen and a free spirit. Like Erin, Caoimhe was shaping up to be an excellent athlete, but it was Erin who craved success. Inés often wondered how much of that was down to losing her father at such a pivotal age – George had been Erin's biggest champion.

As they walked towards the ring, Inés cast her eyes over the other competitors. There were only a few good showjumpers attempting to make the team, all dressed in the standard garb of cream jodhpurs and black fitted blazers. As long as Erin had a good run of it today, she'd be likely to win.

'The turn looks tight between jumps three and four. Remember that shortcut through the flowerpots to give yourself a better angle,' Inés advised as they surveyed the course.

There was always a shortcut hidden among the obstacles. And those savvy enough to spot it could claim an advantage. They'd already walked around the arena before the competition began to plan their strategy, though they hadn't actually walked the planned shortcut. They didn't want to give any hints to the other competitors.

'That'll shave off half a second.' Erin nodded as she sat atop Baby, cooing at him in an attempt to calm her own nerves as much as his.

Inés took in a deep, calming breath, about to begin her usual morale-boosting speech to Erin. She drew on her memories of being ringside with Erin and George, and tried her best to mimic what he would have said. His calm fortitude had lifted Erin and made competitions exciting rather than nerve-wracking for their daughter, and masked his nerves effortlessly in the process. But Inés could sense his emotions better than anyone. They'd spent their late teenage years together at university and married young. When any of their daughters were doing something amazing, his pride and nervousness showed in the little squeezes he gave Inés' hand while watching them perform.

A drink was suddenly thrust under Inés' nose by Lady Elizabeth de Bohun. 'Here you are, dear. You look like you need one of these.' Lady Elizabeth's shrill voice and perfect diction echoed around the warm-up ring.

'Oh, I never say no to a drink,' Inés replied politely, accepting a plastic cup holding an inch of golden liquid. She threw a knowing look at Erin, who looked both amused and distracted.

'And of course I wouldn't forget you, Reenie, sweetheart. Here you go. This will give you a boost.' With a shake of her wrist, Elizabeth offered her a swig from a hip flask.

Annoyed but not shocked at this behaviour, Inés gently guided the flask away.

Erin looked towards the ring, worrying her lower lip with her teeth. 'You'll get us kicked out of the competition if anyone sees her having that before jumping!'

'AHHH!' Elizabeth screeched, igniting a chain reaction of chaos culminating in an up-until-now dozing pony bolting straight towards a barrier which separated the spectators from the competitors. Jumping out of the ring, the pony ditched its rider in the process for good measure. Lady Elizabeth seemed blissfully unaware.

'You've caught me!' Slurping at the flask herself, she continued: 'Just knocking the star rider out of the competition. Can you blame me?' Her voice was so loud, Inés thought even God must have had a headache. She wondered how much Elizabeth had already drunk from her hip flask.

'My name is Erin. Reenie sounds like a nineteen forties housewife,' said Erin, keeping her gaze fixed on the rider performing her round.

Elizabeth beamed at her. 'Oh, I think Reenie is such a sweet name. It suits you. Anyway, best of luck, dear. I'll see you soon, Inés, darling.' After a flourish of air kisses, Elizabeth wandered off to crash another innocent bystander's conversation. Mother and daughter exchanged a glance and simultaneously burst out laughing.

'Oh mum, she's so horrendous. "Reenie", honestly.'

'There's no ill will in her,' Inés chuckled. 'She's a little overbearing, perhaps.'

'Ben's a little shit.'

'I can't argue with that, but stop swearing.'

For the second time, Inés attempted to launch into her pep talk. She was interrupted again – this time by a tall, awkward looking boy a little younger than Erin.

'Hey, guys,' he said, lolloping over to them. Erin's face lit up. Tristan was a regular on the circuit and – in Inés' opinion – a thoroughly nice boy. He and Erin had been friends for years. Even when pitted against each other in the ring, they exchanged sly winks or smiles, or tried to psyche the other out in good humour. He was an incredibly talented rider too, his natural awkwardness vanishing as soon as he was on a horse. Inés would put money on him making it into the British team.

'Tristan!' Erin replied with delight. 'I wondered if we'd see you. I see you're having a great season, as usual.'

Tristan shrugged modestly.

'Erin Cullen,' came a voice over the tannoy.

'Gotta go.' Erin, her face serious now, was off like a bullet, her friend forgotten. Inés and Tristan watched her depart.

'I hope she does well. Pony's looking good,' Tristan commented before leaving to attend to his own horse. Inés waved him goodbye and then turned to a man standing beside her whose child was currently shouting demands of him.

'Whose pony just jumped into the crowd?' Inés inquired.

'Oh,' the man's eyes darted between his daughter, who was struggling to control her pony, and Inés. 'Um, Maria … Ing … Inglefield's.' He managed eventually. 'That's her daughter, Chelsea, who just hit the deck.' The man then carried on shouting directions at his, by now, out-of-control daughter.

Inés hurried to the ring where Erin would soon be appearing, thinking about the effortless snap of the startled pony's jump. Ever the businesswoman, she had a thirst for a good deal, and this was the perfect opportunity.

She pulled her phone out of Erin's oversized pink sports bag, and within a few minutes Inés' offer of half its worth had been grudgingly accepted. *That pony's going places,* Inés thought.

Erin jumped the first three fences beautifully, but at the sharp turn between the flowers, Million Dollar Baby's shoe came flying off and stuck itself neatly into an official's car bonnet, positioned just outside the arena. Inés let out her breath in a rush of disappointment for her daughter. 'Fuck,' she muttered under her breath.

With her pony lame, Erin had no choice but to retire from the round. With a sporting nod to the judge, she dismounted and led Baby out of the ring. Another chance at the qualifiers lost. Inés rushed to comfort her, but as soon as they locked eyes, Erin raised a hand.

'It's all right, mum,' she sighed. 'It can't be helped.' But the rising disappointment in her eyes told a different story.

Inés laid a hand on her shoulder. 'It was bad luck,' she said softly. 'The round was perfect until that point; you were doing amazingly, in fact. We'll call the farrier first thing on Monday morning and get him fixed up in time for next weekend. You'll have another chance then – and this time you'll qualify. He's a gold medal pony, we both know it, just a little sensitive in the feet.'

Erin nodded but didn't speak as they packed away, knowing that the team selectors would be watching – and judging. Although they'd understand the bad luck of losing a shoe halfway through a round, they might not want a horse with such poor feet on their squad. Gossip would soon travel around the equestrian circuit and end up with phone calls offering commiserations, which would make Erin feel even worse.

Chapter Two

On the way home, despite her mother's attempts to engage her in conversation and lighten the mood, Erin stared gloomily out of the window, answering in grunts. Finally, after an hour, Inés put some Prince on, turned the volume up as loud as it would go and sang. Erin looked at her with a slight smile playing around the corners of her mouth, and by the next song was joining in and laughing. When they'd finally arrived home her mood had lightened.

'Here we are, back at the madhouse,' Inés said.

'Speak for yourself,' Erin retorted.

The grooms took over the lorry and busied themselves with Baby. Inés and Erin approached their home, the lavender-lined path filled the air with perfume. George had planted these himself. Although he wasn't much of a gardener and usually killed anything he tried to plant, these had survived long enough to become established in the dry ground. The scent of the bushes welcomed Inés, and she could *see* George leaning against the door frame with a smile on his face, arms folded over a well-toned body and always in a suit. That was one of the things she loved about him. He took such pride in his appearance;

his look was timeless, always in tailored suits and Italian shoes, even at the shows where he would become covered in mud and horse hair.

They walked around the house and stepped through the back door into the large, flag stoned kitchen to be immediately greeted by Spanky, their golden retriever, and a gang of sighthounds the family had collected over the years. Inés was sure there was one dog in the pack that neither George nor she had acquired, but somehow it had ended up with them. Of course, Inés suspected one of her daughters was responsible for the cuckoo in the nest, but never pursued the matter – she'd only have agreed to yet another dog, anyway. Their house was a place for menageries and any stray looking for love. The dogs ran circles in excitement, nuzzling at Inés' and Erin's knees as they bustled into the grand dark wood hallway. Erin hunched down and buried her face in Spanky's fur and he gave her a lick, sensing that all wasn't well. Inés tactfully left Erin to pet the dog, then went to hang up her coat and dump the competition laundry in the dingy utility room.

The room was steeped in dog beds. Their numerous blankets were bundled into a corner and seemed to be moving. Inés pulled at an old duvet one of the dogs used as a bed and found her youngest daughter, Lily, giggling underneath. 'I'm making a den.'

Inés pulled her up into a big cuddle, stroking Lily's hair, which now smelled like old dog. 'You need a bath,' Inés insisted.

Their home was a vast Tudor house in the Surrey Hills that had enough room for Inés, her five daughters and her mother, Alice. Although it had been great to have an extra pair of hands on board since George's death, Alice could cause Inés as much trouble as the children. Lately, she kept insisting she'd heard someone creeping around the house late at night and was convinced they either had a recurring burglar who never seemed to steal anything, or a ghost. Inés worried that Alice had a touch of dementia – or perhaps it was the Irish whiskey she insisted on drinking so late at night that invoked the notion of a poltergeist.

Their home was shared with the girls' nanny, Jane, who lived in a small annex adjacent to the utility room. She'd been part of the family since Erin was newborn. This afforded Jane the right to tell anyone off – including Inés – when they were out of line. She'd come to Inés and George after her previous employers' children had gone to college. She still kept in touch with the children she used to care for, all these years later. Jane was a kind, private woman who never talked about her life before coming to the Cullen family. Inés liked that she wasn't a gossip, but she did sometimes wonder what secrets lay in her guarded past.

Jane was a homely, kind woman who loved the girls – she'd been a godsend. Alice, however, had other ideas, and was always criticising her, making jibes at her cooking (which was divine) and childcare skills (which couldn't be better). Inés regularly had to ask Alice to back off, and she'd do so reluctantly for a few months until Jane once again did something that annoyed her. Inés put this down to Jane's presence in the children's lives, years before Alice had made her way over from the old country, and dismissed her concerns as something her mother would have to get over.

Dinner was ready when they made their way to the dining room. The walls were panelled with a rich wood, and complementary red and gold wallpaper crossed the ceiling. The huge room was filled with mismatched oak furniture that bit back when you stubbed your toe against it. This was Inés' favourite room as dinner was one of the few times of the day that everyone sat together and the room's lack of a TV meant the family had no choice but to talk to each other.

Fiadh and Imogen sat on either side of Inés, happily stuffing their faces with sausage and mash. They had come along after Caoimhe and were a quiet, studious pair who often seemed wrapped up in their own self-contained unit. Identical twins, they finished each other's sentences and always fell ill at the same time. Although Inés had known she might have twins as they ran in both sides of the family, it had still come as a shock when the scan had revealed two babies instead of one. She remembered George's face, shocked and strangely proud, as though it were evidence of his manly prowess.

At the end of the table sat Lily, her youngest, next to Jane. Now six, Lily had been a surprise baby, too. Inés had intended to stop at three, but life clearly had other plans, and she wouldn't have had it any other way. The girls were her world and had kept her going after George's sudden death. Lily was barely a toddler when the tragedy happened and it saddened Inés that she'd never truly know her father.

Lily was playing with her peas, putting them in orderly straight lines across her plate. Inés smiled as she watched her. Lily was a quirky thing, almost fey. Alice often referred to old Irish tales of changelings when talking about Lily, but Alice saw signs, curses and folktales everywhere she cared to look.

'Lily, don't play with your food,' Jane admonished gently. Lily pouted at her, mumbling something barely audible that sounded like a different language.

'What are you saying, sweetheart?' Inés asked.

Caoimhe grinned. 'She's made her own language up,' she said, 'and she replies to herself in it. It's clever really, mum.'

'Yes, I suppose it is,' Inés mused. Jane looked relieved, as if worried Inés wouldn't understand Lily's latest eccentricity. Inés had become short with the girls, Jane, and Alice, occasionally over the most innocuous of things after George's passing, but was coming through the other side and getting back to her old self once again. Her plate was always too full and sometimes she slipped up, but her bark was worse than her bite and the children seemed to know this, so they didn't take too much notice of her admonishments.

As they sat down, she glanced at Erin, who looked subdued again. Inés winced as Caoimhe, helping herself to the bowl of potatoes, asked: 'So how did it go, Erin? You qualified, right?'

'No,' said Erin shortly.

'She did amazingly,' Inés jumped in before Caoimhe could ask Erin to explain. 'Million Dollar Baby lost a shoe, but before that she was flying around the course beautifully. It was just bad luck.'

'Like last week was an "off day"', Erin mumbled, staring down at her plate.

Caoimhe jabbed her in the side. 'Cheer up,' she said gaily. 'You've still got next week. It'll be fine, you'll see.' Caoimhe's attempt to reassure her sister fell on deaf ears, but Inés hoped Caoimhe's warm empathetic efforts were appreciated by Erin. They were very close and though rivalry was bound to crop up between them now and again, given that they were so competitive, they were fiercely loyal to each other. Caoimhe tried again. 'At least that big spot on your face has cleared up. *Thank the Lord for his mercy.*'

The children fell about laughing at her impression of their grandma. All except Erin. She didn't reply, and Inés felt her heart ache for her oldest daughter. *If only she'd stop being so hard on herself.*

Alice had taken her dinner to her room, which she often did these days. Her mother was starting to show her age. Inés had had a tumultuous relationship with her mother as a young woman; a fire that had been reignited after Alice moved with the family. But the thought of her mother returning to Ireland and leaving them terrified

Inés. Alice tired more easily nowadays, although she would never admit it, and had endless patience with the children, even when she shouldn't. Inés was sure that was the root of Alice's annoyance with Jane; she felt usurped by the younger outsider.

After dinner, Inés helped Jane clear away, then made sure the kids were bathed and in their rooms. She left Jane to put Lily to bed so she could get on with some work. Inés kissed Lily, wishing she didn't have to delegate bedtime, but she had to come to terms with these sacrifices if she wanted to remain successful and give the girls a high standard of living. She smiled gratefully at Jane as she left the room with Lily, reminding herself that she was going out in London on Monday night after work. It was the anniversary of George's death, and it had become a tradition for her and her best friends, Tabatha – who everyone referred to as Tabby – and Chris, to drink a toast to him in what had been their favourite wine bar.

Four years, Inés thought as she stacked the dishwasher. It had been such a long time.

Chapter Three

'Four years is a long time, darling,' Chris said as he sipped on his Moët. 'When are you going to get back on the horse, so to speak?'

The friends sat in a cosy booth at one of their old haunts, El Pirata in Mayfair. They liked this place as the music wasn't too loud to have a conversation and there was a great tapas menu to stop patrons who'd come straight out of work from getting drunk.

'I don't go anywhere to meet anyone,' Inés sighed. 'I'm so busy with work and the girls and the horses – the twins are turning into real hellraisers. Besides, I'm not sure I want anyone.'

'There must be some nice men at CCM?' Tabby interjected, stroking her stomach and sipping her mocktail. She was finally pregnant after a year of trying and, at five months, beginning to show. The sperm donor, she'd been assured by the clinic, had good healthy genes and would make an excellent (though absent) father. Inés was excited that one of her friends was also going to be a parent, and felt protective of Tabby.

'I tried two years ago,' Inés reminded her. 'When I attempted to date Boring Bobby. Then when I decided I wasn't interested, he practically followed me around at work with those dreadful moony eyes of his. It was a relief when he was transferred abroad.'

'Yes, but you only went out with him because we nagged you to accept.'

'Like we're nagging her now?' Chris laughed, placing a hand on his perfectly styled hair. 'She's right though, Inés. You're too fussy. Honestly, you need to get laid. It'd blow those cobwebs out if nothing else.'

Chris worked as a senior financial advisor at a strait-laced, dusty old law firm. Inés loved him dearly. They'd been friends since university and he often came to stay with her and the girls when he needed a break from the stress of London – and somewhere he could be himself for a few days. The girls adored him, and George had been fond of him, too. Tabby had been married to an old friend of George's until she'd discovered him in bed with another woman. Since then, Inés and Tabby's bond had grown into a strong friendship. Her divorce had been messy and she'd been so hurt that she'd never been with a man since.

Inés couldn't imagine life without either of them.

The atmosphere in El Pirata was calm, even as it filled up with young professionals. Inés looked at them, dressed in workwear and happy to party on a Monday evening. She remembered the buzz of going out after work as a junior, feeling the electric pulse of London, like you were on a ride to conquer the world, a ride you couldn't get off. El Pirata made Inés feel younger than her years as she thought of the evenings she, George and Chris had spent there after work. Memories of George, mixed with the buzz of the bar, filled her with melancholy.

'Aren't you off to Spain soon?' Chris said. 'Maybe a young Spanish waiter is what you need.'

'It depends on whether Erin qualifies for Spain this weekend. I hope so. She needs this. But I don't think she'd be impressed if I started sneaking off with the waiters. Besides, toy boys aren't my thing. I need someone – sophisticated. Worldly,' she said wistfully.

Chris crossed his legs carefully, showing off his perfectly tailored checked trousers. 'How about that dreamy teacher at the girls' school?' he continued, his accent clipped and clear. 'The one I met last time I stayed at yours.'

'Mr Taylor? He's the girls' headmaster and wears brown suits ... not my type.'

'You are a snob,' Chris said, affectionately patting her leg.

'I am not!' Inés protested with a sarcastic flick of her sleek bob. She thought about Mr Taylor. She supposed he was handsome, with curly dark hair and kind hazel eyes that anyone with a pulse could get lost in. But no, definitely not her type. Inés favoured men with means and those who matched her level of business prowess; preferably with a high-powered job and jet-setting lifestyle. She couldn't imagine a teacher fitting in with her life at all.

'Nothing wrong with standards,' Tabby said. 'I made sure the bump's sperm donor was from a high-income bracket.'

'Seems pointless,' Chris said. 'It's not as though you can

tap him up for child maintenance.' A wicked smile crept across his face. 'Besides, that's what the clinic told you. For all you know, a bored caretaker swapped some samples in a broom closet.'

Inés laughed, then sipped her Dark and Stormy, feeling the warm fuzzy glow of two drinks and her friends' company. *They were right*, she reflected. *It had been too long.*

She wasn't sure where the years had gone. Although she'd grieved for her husband, they hadn't been madly in love at the end. The spark had gone a long time ago. They'd been best friends and companions and parented together very successfully. However, they'd agreed that breaking up was not an option, and their children would benefit from having parents who stayed married. Just before George's fatal accident they'd even started discussing the possibility of some form of open relationship as a way to keep their marriage intact while allowing them a bit of fun. Whether that would have worked or not, she'd never know. After the accident, Inés' interest in men had dwindled drastically.

Her friends were right. It was time she had a fling. She cast her eye around the bar. Tabby noticed and pointed to a younger man standing with his friends. He was handsome in a city-boy way, although he was wearing a badly cut suit. Inés wrinkled her nose.

'Too young,' she said. 'And look at that suit!'

'Snob,' chorused Chris and Tabby simultaneously. Inés threw her napkin at them and they enjoyed the rest of their evening.

Chapter Four

The following Friday, Inés had her end of the month half-day. As London grew smaller in the rear-view mirror of her Porsche, she looked forward to collecting the younger girls and spending quality time with them. Inés couldn't wait to hear about the messy things they'd got themselves into that day, or which teacher the twins had tricked by swapping identities. The twins were already begging Inés to become regular boarders at their prep school, and although she wasn't ready to let go of them yet, it wouldn't be long before she gave in to their demands. After that, it would just be Lily rattling around the house during weekdays.

How long would that last?

The crater that'd formed in Inés' heart when Erin started to board widened with each passing year and as every daughter decided to do the same. For the girls it was an adventure; they came back with stories of sneaking into the kitchens for midnight feasts – like one big slumber party. It would have been selfish not to let them have their fun, but that didn't stop the empty feeling in the house during term time. Erin and Caoimhe were in a separate college to the younger girls and would usually get on the school bus, though it wouldn't be long before Erin was behind the wheel. The thought sent a shudder down her spine as she cruised through her tree-lined driveway, halting with a skid by the postbox. Before continuing to the school, she'd decided to kill some time and go through her letters. When she opened her mailbox she felt a chill of recognition at the name printed on the large envelope. It wasn't addressed to her.

George.

Odd, after all this time. Inés opened it, feeling a sense of foreboding as she recognised the logo for HM Revenue & Customs. She got back into the car, having the sudden sense that whatever this was, she needed to sit down for it. She slid out the letter, frowning as she read it through.

They owed money.

Or rather, George did, on the company consultancy business he'd owned with his friend, Kent. Inés had been a shareholder. Inés frowned, reading the letter again and trying to make sense of the six-figure bill. Why was this coming now? Why hadn't Kent called her to tell her to expect it, and why was George's name on the letter? She'd thought Kent had resolved the business' financial problems after George's death.

Confusion swam in her mind. *Where was George? Why wasn't he here? It wasn't fair.* The letter slipped from her fingers and into the freshly vacuumed footwell. She felt the uncomfortable beginnings of a lump in her throat. Feeling like a child, she allowed herself to cry. Just for a few minutes, before pulling herself back together. She tugged down the sun visor and opened the mirror. Her mascara was smudged. Using the back of her hand to clean herself up, she whispered to her reflection, 'What mess have you left for me now?'

She paused and took a breath. Perhaps there was some kind of mistake, she reasoned, pulling herself together and applying Dior's new pale pink lipstick. It wouldn't be the first time that HM Revenue & Customs had miscalculated. *This was a whopper of a miscalculation.* She slipped the letter into her bag, resolving to call her accountant and Kent the next day, then restarted the engine.

Oakfield Prep was a small private school, well worth the extortionate amount of money she spent on fees. It stood in the middle of the rolling hills of Surrey. Its Gothic-style building nestled snugly in the surrounding countryside and was hidden away from the well-trodden tracks of the main roads.

As she reached the juniors entrance to wait for Lily, she saw the headmaster, Raphael Taylor, standing there with his dark brown hair falling over one eye. Remembering her conversation with Chris and Tabby earlier in the week, Inés felt her cheeks flush. *He was handsome*, she admitted, sneaking a peek at him. He had cheekbones to die for and towered above the milling mothers. As she got closer to him, Inés noticed how sensual his mouth was. A mouth that longed to be kissed. He seemed completely unaware of his beauty and was quiet, even self-effacing at times. As she'd told her friends, he wasn't her type at all.

Definitely not.

She felt pleasantly warm when he noticed her and smiled, his eyes alight as they met hers. 'Afternoon, Inés. How are things in London?' he said, smiling broadly.

'Busy as ever,' she said. There was an awkward silence as Inés wondered what to say.

'How is everything at the yard?' 'Raff' tried again and Inés realised he wasn't simply being polite but was actively trying to engage her in conversation. It was starting to rain and she ducked under the porch of the entrance. Following her lead, some of the other mothers and nannies crowded in, pushing her closer to Raff than she'd intended.

'Oh, really well, actually. Erin has a qualifier tomorrow – it's her last chance to make it to Spain, so she was a bag of nerves this morning.'

Raff looked concerned. He'd come on board as headmaster in Erin's last year – the year they'd lost George. Inés remembered him telling her and George how bright Erin was, but also that she was a perfectionist who grew anxious at the prospect of failure. *He'd been right about one thing*, she thought, remembering last Saturday and hoping tomorrow would have a better outcome and end Erin's run of bad luck.

'She always was a worrier – unlike Caoimhe. They're like chalk and cheese, aren't they?'

'Definitely,' Inés nodded. They fell silent again until Raff cleared his throat awkwardly.

'Ah, that sounds like Lily's class now,' he said. Then his attention was taken up by a teacher and Inés turned towards a tsunami of children spilling out of class. As usual, Lily was the only one who couldn't stay in line, fidgeting and singing to herself and then breaking ranks as soon as she saw Inés, barrelling into her arms. Inés picked her up and planted a kiss on her cheek before setting her back down and taking her hand. 'Come on, let's go and meet your sisters.' She looked back as they walked off and saw Raff watching her. He raised a hand in goodbye and she gave him a wave, feeling silly.

'Mr Taylor likes you, mum,' Lily said, pulling Inés' hand as she skipped along ahead.

'Well, I suppose he has to be friendly with all the parents,' Inés said diplomatically. Lily shook her head, her curls bouncing.

'No, I mean he likes you *especially*. He always comes out on the Fridays when you come to pick us up.'

'Really? I'm sure that's not the case.'

'It is,' Lily said, who then let go of her hand and ran towards Fiadh and Imogen who were approaching from the other end of the grounds. The twins were arm in arm, the different coloured ribbons in their hair the only thing that enabled most people to tell them apart. Imogen's cheekbones were ever so slightly sharper and Fiadh had a small birthmark on her upper arm, but even Inés sometimes got them mixed up.

She kissed them both and they walked towards the car while Lily chattered away. Back home, Jane had a light tea waiting for them all, sandwiches, a homemade Victoria sponge and a pot of tea. Inés cut a piece of cake and poured herself a tea then sat at the huge kitchen island, while the girls ran to get changed out of their uniforms.

'Jane, you're a star,' Inés said through a mouthful of cake. 'This is just what I need.' She gave a contented sigh, tucking into more of the delicious cake.

'Well, I had a quiet afternoon and I haven't baked for a while,' Jane said, sitting opposite her. 'Are you going to the party tonight?'

Inés had almost forgotten the party. Elizabeth had phoned her a few days ago, inviting her to 'a little soirée, darling,' taking Inés' non-committal murmur as a definite yes. The de Bohun's parties were sometimes fun, providing Elizabeth didn't insist on dragging Inés around to meet every eligible bachelor in the room, who were usually insufferable bores.

'I don't know. I may pop in for an hour, after the girls have gone to bed. But I'm out next week as well, with Tabby and Chris for the opening of that new club. Are you sure it's not too much?'

'Oh, that sounds like fun. When are you going?'

'I am pretty sure it's next weekend,' Inés said uncertainly. She wasn't convinced she wanted to go, but she'd promised Tabby and Chris after a few too many. It had seemed like a good idea at the time, but now she was beginning to feel the pull of staying at home.

Jane waved a hand. 'Of course not. Besides, you have to get back into the swing of a social life again. You can't just go out with Tabby and Chris every few months, forever.'

Inés smiled. Alice would have exploded at Jane for

talking this way to Inés, but Inés was used to it. Being told what to do occasionally was a welcome change from having to be the decision maker.

'Go and let your hair down,' Jane insisted.

Inés sipped her tea thoughtfully. *Jane's right.* What with putting the finishing touches to a big contract at work, the girls' various competitions and commitments and her trying to spend quality time with them, her social life had dwindled. A couple of nights out would do her good.

'Okay,' she decided. 'I suppose it will give me a chance to wear the black cocktail dress I bought at the Milan shows last year.'

Just then, Erin and Caoimhe came in, soaking from the rain. Caoimhe laughed as she shook her hair like a dog, sending raindrops spraying across Erin, who shrieked. 'Stop it will you! I'm already soaked.' She turned to Inés. 'Mum, can Charlie come round for dinner?'

Again? Inés thought but didn't say. Charlie was their neighbour's son, and while he seemed to be coming over for dinner with the girls more and more often, Inés was glad they'd become friends. At fifteen, Charlie was between Caoimhe and Erin in age and got on well with them both. He was a pleasant boy who never seemed to get into any trouble, if a little shy. His father, Bert, owned the adjacent farm and was a hard, gruff man who'd resisted Inés' attempts over the years to be neighbourly, as well as rebutting her planning permission applications for seemingly no other reason than spite. Luckily, Inés' financial skills were put to good use by another council member.

Permissions were granted for Inés to extend her house and farm. Bert's second wife, Lois, didn't look to be much older than Erin and was as uncommunicative as a plump house cat. Inés guessed their home was an unfriendly place; no wonder Charlie preferred to be here. He'd wanted to board at his all-boys' school, but his father wouldn't hear of it.

'Yes, of course,' she said, glancing at her work phone. The company would stop Erin from worrying about tomorrow, which could only be a good thing.

'Thanks,' Erin chirped, running off upstairs. Caoimhe sat at the table and helped herself to a fistful of cake, just as Lily came back dressed in her unicorn onesie and climbed into Inés' lap.

'Can you get a plate? And the onesie is for after your bath, Lily.'

'Don't want a bath,' Lily said firmly. 'I got wet in the rain.'

'The rain doesn't wash you, you dope,' Caoimhe said.

'It does. It's like a shower.' Lily stuck her tongue out at her older sister and although Inés reprimanded her, she had to suppress a smile.

Later, after dinner, they sat in the TV room watching a comedy film. Charlie was there, sitting with Caoimhe on the oversized beanbag George had bought for Inés when she'd been pregnant with the twins. Lily cuddled into Inés, still in her unicorn onesie, and her eyes started to droop. Inés lifted her up carefully and carried her up to her room, reading to her until she was sound asleep.

Inés laid a gentle kiss on her daughter's forehead, who

in a deep sleep looked perfectly angelic. These had always been her favourite moments, right from when Erin had been small. George's too. In fact, they'd fought to be the one to put the girls to bed. She felt a pang of loss, like the ache of a wound long thought healed, wishing he'd been able to see the girls grow up. Although she'd worked hard to give them everything, she couldn't give them their father back.

She sat up, telling herself not to be maudlin. It was what it was, there was no changing it, and she'd made the best of things. George would have been proud of her success and of how the girls were growing up. Lately though, she was starting to feel lonely. It would be good to have a man around now and then, if only to accompany her to things like Elizabeth's 'little soirée'. At least then Elizabeth wouldn't insist on trying to play Cupid.

I'd better get ready, she thought and headed into her bedroom. She had a quick shower, then expertly tonged her ebony hair. Her hair colour highlighted her large green eyes and high cheekbones beautifully.

She applied foundation, highlighter, a sweep of bronzer and some tasteful false lashes, pulled on her dressing gown and went downstairs to sit with the girls. Fiadh and Imogen went up to their room after the film finished, and Caoimhe and Charlie started playing a board game, while Erin had her head stuck in a novel. Jane had gone to her annex and Alice was dozing in the armchair. Inés smiled contentedly, feeling a wave of gratitude. Yes, she missed having a partner but mostly her life was great, and her family supplied her with the company she needed.

She noticed dark circles under Charlie's eyes. 'Are you feeling okay, Charlie?' she asked with the authority that only a mother can command.

'Oh, yeah. Just been cramming for exams. So, lots of late nights.' His awkward smile was unconvincing, but Inés decided against pressing the issue further in front of the whole family.

I will have to pick a better time to talk to him, Inés thought. Although nothing had been said, she had a bad feeling when she looked at Charlie. Like she was dismissing a lost dog at the side of the road.

Back upstairs she wriggled into her cocktail dress, pleased it still fitted her slender figure perfectly, and turned to one side and then the other in the mirror, smoothing the silky material over her hips. Maybe one of Elizabeth's bachelors would actually be promising tonight. She applied her favourite red lipstick, grabbed her little black bag, and headed down the stairs to call a taxi. Stathum Manor was within walking distance in wellies, but not in five-inch heels.

The de Bohun's butler met her from the parked taxi and ushered her through the huge wooden doors. A young and buff waiter, obviously hired for the occasion, hurried over to supply her with a flute of expensive champagne. This was Elizabeth's idea of a 'little soirée'.

The grand hall was filled with family heirlooms of marble and bronze, with high ceilings affording plenty of room for the gargantuan crystal chandelier that hung there.

Inés sipped her drink, thankful she'd made an effort for the occasion. She admired the rich tapestries along the walls, visualising them thoughtfully in her own house. *Perhaps I should look into local auctions.*

Elizabeth spotted her and hurried over, leaving the man she'd been in conversation with standing alone mid-sentence. Although she could only see him from behind, he seemed vaguely familiar to Inés, but her view was soon blocked.

'Oh darling, I'm so glad you came! There are so many people I simply have to introduce you to!'

'Here we go,' Inés murmured. Elizabeth was dressed in a crimson cocktail dress that was a tad too tight on her full thighs and clashed horribly with her peach lipstick. In spite of her wealth, poor Elizabeth could use some fashion advice.

'I'm so sorry about poor Erin and her horse,' Elizabeth gushed. 'She must be so terribly disappointed.'

Inés bristled. 'She has a chance to qualify again tomorrow, and I'm sure she'll be fine. She's an excellent jumper and I know Million Dollar Baby will come through.'

'Oh, of course, she's very good … a tad overcautious though, don't you think, Inés?' Inés was about to retort in Erin's defence when Elizabeth continued, 'But then I'm so used to Benjamin, who's such a brave rider.' Inés suspected this line of conversation was more to do with

Elizabeth's inability to stop talking rather than any genuine slight against Erin.

A complete show-off, you mean, Inés thought uncharitably, wondering why on earth she'd agreed to come.

'He'll be thrilled if Erin ends up on the team with him.'

Inés, who knew Erin and Ben had no love for each other, smiled warily. She was about to take her leave and get started on the canapés when Elizabeth linked her arm through hers, her voice now low and chummy.

'Let's not talk horses tonight. You simply must come and meet Lord Byron-Taylor.'

A lord? Inés braced herself for a stuffy old bore, as Elizabeth steered her towards the man she'd been speaking to when Inés had arrived.

'Lord Byron-Taylor?' Elizabeth cooed, making a point of emphasising his title, 'this is my dear friend and neighbour, Inés.'

The man turned round with an embarrassed smile, and Inés' mouth fell open.

'Please, Elizabeth, call me Raff,' said Inés' children's headmaster. Then he noticed Inés and coloured bright red.

'Lord?' Inés echoed with surprise. Raff shifted uncomfortably, looking as though he wished the ground would swallow him up. 'I try not to use my title,' he said, shooting a look at Elizabeth, who tittered innocently. 'It's very old and goes back generations.'

'It's such an interesting story,' Elizabeth cut in. 'Raff's father was a terrible scoundrel and gambled much of the family money away, then the rest was swallowed up in inheritance tax – such a travesty.'

Inés' jaw couldn't quite close. Her children's headmaster was a peer of the realm? And this whole time she hadn't known? She thought of the conversation she'd had with her friends about him and how they'd love to hear this piece of gossip.

'That's interesting,' she said quietly, not taking her eyes off Raff, who looked more handsome than usual in a well-tailored suit and with his usually unruly hair carefully styled. Chris would call her a terrible snob, but she couldn't help but see him in a whole new light. 'I feel silly that I was so unaware, but I don't believe the girls know, either? I'm sure they'd have mentioned it.'

'Well, it doesn't seem relevant to discuss with pupils,' Raff began, before Elizabeth cut in again with a shriek, raising one perfectly manicured hand to her mouth in an exaggerated gesture.

'Oh, my goodness. I should have realised! You teach, don't you? So, you're the twins' headmaster? And here's me, so excited to introduce you and you already know each other! Now I do feel silly! Well, I'll leave you two to chat.' Elizabeth was gone, rushing over to a young couple who'd just arrived, her loud voice braying across the room. Inés and Raff stood in an awkward silence.

'I never mentioned it … I've never wanted it to distract from my role at the school.' Raff said.

'Not at all,' said Inés. 'It's completely your business. I'm so sorry you lost your fortune like that. It seems so unfair.'

Raff shrugged. 'The title was probably gained unfairly. I suppose it's fitting.'

Inés couldn't help but feel intrigued.

'There wasn't much of a fortune left after my father's gambling and some ill-advised investments by my uncle,' he admitted. 'Our manor had to be sold for the tax, but I made enough from the sale to buy myself a cottage and live comfortably.'

'Oh, but you still teach?' Inés asked, wondering why on earth anyone with means would choose to look after a school full of small children every day when he must surely have contacts in the City if he wanted a career.

'It's my vocation,' he said simply. 'Something I've always wanted to do. When I was at Eton, there was a teacher who inspired me, and I've never forgotten the difference he made to us. Also, it would greatly annoy my father if he's looking down at us – or perhaps I should say *up* at us.'

Inés, humbled by Raff's altruism, wanted nothing more than to spend the evening in his company. She felt warm and familiar and easy in his presence and searched for something else to discuss, not wanting to let go of the moment. 'How do you know Elizabeth?' she asked.

'Oh, I don't really,' he said, as a younger, blonde woman with a mouthful of canapés joined them and linked her arm with Raff's. 'She's a friend of Clarissa's.'

Clarissa gave Inés a wave and Inés smiled tightly, suddenly feeling deflated and conscious of her singleness. Somehow, she'd never pictured the headmaster with a date or girlfriend, but why wouldn't he have one? And lords, she imagined, even less-wealthy ones, were likely never short of a date.

'Nice to meet you,' she said politely to Clarissa, who was clinging to Raff almost territorially.

'You too,' Clarissa replied in a horsey tone that reminded her of Elizabeth.

'So, how long have you known El –' Inés began, but was interrupted again.

'Darling, you must come and try this food. The chef is simply divine. Elizabeth always hires the best.' She all but dragged Raff away. He looked back over his shoulder at Inés apologetically, and Inés smiled sadly and then turned to look around the room, hoping to spot someone she knew, or at least another glass of Dom Pérignon.

'Inés? Is it you?' A smooth, rich, Texan voice glided to her ears. She recognised it instantly. Smiling in surprise, Inés turned to face him.

'Kent! How lovely to see you. It's been such a long time.'

Nearly two years, in fact, ever since Kent had bought Inés out as a shareholder in the consultancy company he owned with her husband. Seeing Kent brought back a rush of memories. He'd been one of George's best friends as well as his business partner and had been best man at their wedding and godfather to Erin. When George was alive, Kent was a regular fixture in their life.

He'd been fantastic in the aftermath too, helping out where he could and taking Inés out for lunch when the demands of being newly widowed with five children, the youngest only a baby, got too much for her. There'd been a time when Inés had thought they were getting close – too close.

She'd pulled away, her emotions too raw to entertain the idea of dating George's friend. More than that: Kent had been there when George had fallen overboard on that ill-fated night. At first, their shared grief had allowed them to bond, but as the years went by and Inés moved out of the stage of mourning, Kent's presence became a painful reminder. And so, over the last couple of years, she'd let their friendship slide. Seeing him now, Inés realised how much she'd missed him.

'You look well,' she said, hoping her voice didn't give away her shock. She noticed how tanned he was as her eyes danced around his face. His dark hair was starting to streak with grey, but it suited him, bringing out the cobalt in his eyes. Inés gulped at her drink as she felt her tummy fizz. Kent's gaze so subtly looked her up and down, lighting up with approval.

'I've just got back from business in Italy. And you, my dear, look even more stunning than I remember.'

He leaned forward and kissed her cheek in polite greeting, leaving her skin tingling under its imprint. Inés felt unsettled, an effect she only now recalled Kent having on her many times before. He'd never been inappropriate or made a move – she'd been his best friend's wife, after all – but there'd always been an undercurrent of desire between them and now, four years after George's death, that seemed to have intensified.

'How are the girls? Erin must be turning into a young lady.'

'Yes, she's sixteen. She will be in sixth form in September.' Inés talked about the girls, particularly Erin and Caoimhe's sporting achievements, and her hopes for them, knowing that Kent was a big sports fan and would be interested. He listened intently, making sympathetic noises when she told him about Erin's last chance at qualifying.

'Do you have a sponsor for her?' he asked.

Inés shook her head.

'Perhaps it's something I should think about,' he mused, and Inés masked her excitement of this idea. A wealthy sponsor like Kent could be a great asset and give Erin a real confidence boost.

She suddenly remembered the letter she'd received. 'It must be fate that our paths crossed today.' She chose her words carefully to pique Kent's interest. 'I was going to phone you tomorrow.' Her words hung in the air as she waited for Kent to take the bait. She wanted him on the back foot in case there was more to this letter than an admin mix-up.

'Oh?' Kent's eyes twinkled. 'Sounds interesting.'

Inés shook her head with a smile. 'Not a social call, I'm afraid. I received a letter from HM Revenue & Customs about tax George owes from the consultancy business. I can't make head nor tail of it.' Allowing herself to sound ignorant, she added: 'I assumed there shouldn't be any-thing owing at all. I'm going to get my accountant to look it over, but I wanted to let you know before I brought more people in. It's a substantial sum.' She paused, giving herself an opportunity to read him, then continued. 'Do you know what it could be about?'

Kent inclined his head. 'I assume it has something to do with that bit of difficulty George was involved in, though I don't know.'

Kent's confession that he'd known something was up while George was still around reassured Inés enough – *for now* – that he was being honest. Though his apparent lack of knowledge about a business he was a partner of niggled at her. But that could wait. If nothing else, Inés was strategic and she could be ruthless if need be.

He added: 'Of course, I haven't seen the letter. Perhaps we should get together over coffee and have a look at it? It will give me a convenient excuse to see you again.'

'Sure, let's meet up and have a chat,' Inés said casually, trying not to sound too eager.

Kent met her gaze and held it. 'I'd like that very much,' he said, his voice suddenly low and intimate. Inés was sure he was more than casually flirting with her, but his tone returned to normal as he chatted about his various business interests and asked her about the yard and her work. He listened intently to her throughout their conversation and they caught up as old friends do. Every time she finished her drink a waiter appeared to top it up. It was *very* good champagne.

'So, has anyone managed to turn the head of the infamous Inés Cullen, then?'

Inés shook her head, his words triggering thoughts of her maiden name. 'The girls, the yard and my career don't leave me much time for dating,' she said lightly.

Kent shook his head. 'I thought you'd be snapped up by now, if you don't mind me saying so. You're a beautiful woman, Inés.'

Inés blushed, feeling flattered. From across the room, she noticed Raff watching her and, for reasons she didn't understand, she let out a tinkling laugh and laid a hand on Kent's arm. 'Thank you, but I could say the same about you. Surely you're not here alone?' She held her hand in place for a touch longer than a friendly pat necessitated.

'Oh, you know me, Inés. I've never met a woman I wanted to settle down with.'

'In all this time?' Inés asked, thinking back through the various girlfriends of Kent's she'd met over the years. She couldn't remember any of them ever lasting more than six months.

'Well, maybe once,' he confessed, 'but then my best friend went and married her.'

Startled by his words, which had a ring of truth, Inés gulped at her champagne. She was beginning to feel tipsy, and so placed her glass on an expensive-looking marquetry table. Jane's cake had made her prematurely full, so she hadn't eaten enough of her dinner.

'Shall we get some food?' she said, rapidly changing the subject. 'There's some wonderful canapés going around and what looks like a lovely buffet in the hall.' Inés looked around to avoid eye contact in the hope Kent wouldn't notice her blush.

'Good idea,' said Kent approvingly. He offered her his arm. Inés hesitated briefly and then took it, walking with him out into the hall where a selection of tapas, caviars and oysters awaited.

'You know these are supposed to be aphrodisiacs?' Kent commented, nudging an oyster.

'I've never understood why,' Inés grimaced. 'Slimy things. I'm not sure anyone really likes them, or whether they pretend in order to impress.'

She was loading her plate when she heard Elizabeth's loud voice coming towards them. 'Why Inés, you know everyone tonight! Is Kent a friend of yours too?'

'I was her best man many years ago,' Kent offered, and Elizabeth shrieked in delight. It soon turned out that Kent knew Guy de Bohun rather than Elizabeth herself, and Guy shortly came over to join them, leaving Inés trapped talking to Elizabeth, who was getting more drunk by the minute. *She's developing a habit*, Inés thought, and wondered if Guy had noticed how much his wife was putting away lately. Judging by the hip flask Elizabeth had been hiding in her pocket at the qualifiers, Inés guessed not.

After a while, Elizabeth tried to usher Inés away again to meet her 'absolutely charming' new friend, Lady something-or-other. Inés glanced at the clock and shook her head in mock regret. 'I should go, I have a busy weekend ahead. But thank you very much for tonight.'

She turned in Kent's direction, hoping to say goodbye

to him, but he was deep in conversation with Guy. She walked away to phone a cab when he appeared by her side. 'Going so soon? I was hoping we could have a nightcap.'

'I have an early start,' Inés said, then added, 'but definitely some other time.'

'That would be fantastic. I'll call you.' He lifted her hand to his lips in what felt like an oddly intimate gesture and then turned back to Guy. Elizabeth had already floated off and Inés went outside to wait for her cab, realising as the cool night air hit her skin just how hot her cheeks were.

As she sat in the back seat of the Uber on her way home, she wondered if Kent would call.

She wondered if she *really* wanted him to.

Back at home, Inés poured herself a glass of antacid and sat in the orangery. Light spilled from the windows on to the box hedges that peppered the lawn, casting beastly shadows on to the grass. The yard was off to the right, out of sight, but she could hear the occasional whinny of a restless horse. They were staying in for the night as rain was expected, though there was no sign of it yet. The moon, heavy and low, cast a pale yellow glow over everything and Inés sat in the cool darkness, deep in thought.

She wasn't sure how seeing Kent had made her feel. Aware of herself as a woman, certainly. It had been a long time since she'd felt desire in anything other than a fleeting sense. She still enjoyed being admired, of course, but that was different. Pulling her cashmere shawl around her more closely, Inés became acutely aware of how long it had been since she'd had sex, and wondered why that was.

George wouldn't have expected her to stay faithful, but the weight of infidelity pressed down on her at the mere thought of another man.

They'd been discussing the possibility of an open marriage not long before he had passed away, aware that the spark between them had long gone. The night Lily was conceived had been the one time they had made love in eighteen months, but they hadn't wanted to separate. Then, suddenly, George hadn't been there anymore. She wondered if she felt a residual guilt that she'd been so ready to break her marriage vows – even with his blessing – and then that terrible accident had happened.

Inés sighed and lifted her glass to her lips again, allowing her deepest fears to take shape in the dark. She'd never told a soul in the years that had passed, not even Chris or Tabby, but after George's death she'd discovered his company was in a lot of debt. Debt that appeared to have been created by George's oversights. He'd been a proud man, and in her darker moments Inés wondered if his fall overboard was deliberate. And as soon as she dismissed the thoughts as foolish, they crept back in as quickly. *George would never have left her and the girls.* He'd been such a stable influence for them all, and she lamented the fact that the girls had lost not only their father but also a great male role model. She drained her glass, pinching her nose. A good night's sleep was what she needed.

Inés shrieked as a crash sounded behind her and jumped to her feet.

'Mother!' Inés stared at Alice who had come through

the orangery door so fast that she'd knocked a chair over. She was holding a rolling pin above her head, which she lowered when she saw Inés.

'Oh, it's you. I saw your shadow and I thought you were an intruder.'

Inés rolled her eyes, pressing a hand to her chest where her heart was going ten to the dozen. 'You scared the shit out of me!' Inés protested. Alice usually laughed at her daughter swearing in her clipped and prim accent, but this time stood fixed to the spot. 'Who else would be sitting in the orangery? I hardly think an intruder would be lazing around helping himself to a drink and the view.'

Alice looked grim as she clutched her rolling pin with her hair under its usual net, 'to keep it soft and healthy' as she so often said. She was wrapped in a huge fluffy dressing gown and green Hunter wellies. Inés felt the corners of her mouth twitch.

Alice snapped, seeing her expression. 'Don't you laugh at me, girl.' She jabbed the rolling pin at Inés like a sewing machine needle following the inflection of her words. 'I'm telling you there's something funny going on in this house. I went to get a glass of water from the kitchen –'

More like a whiskey, Inés thought.

'– and I'm telling you, I saw someone. In the shadows. Creeping. Then I turned the light on and they were gone.'

Inés shook her head. This again. 'Mum, we've checked every single time. There's never any sign of any break in or disturbance. You're jumping at shadows. I mean, honestly, you nearly clobbered me for sitting in my own home.'

'You think I'm going doolally,' Alice accused. 'Seeing things.'

Inés had to fight back another smile as her mother's gesticulations crescendoed.

'Not at all,' Inés protested, although that was exactly what she thought. 'Maybe you're a bit … overtired. Why don't you go and get some sleep?'

Alice tutted and stomped off to signify the conversation had ended. Inés locked up, washed her glass, and went to bed with her laptop. She could probably answer a few emails before she drifted off to sleep. Her company was discussing terms with a Japanese firm and they'd be expecting her to be available at the drop of a hat until everything was sorted.

Chapter Five

This time, her mother managed to get Erin to the qualifier without nearly getting into a tussle with a tree, though Erin would have been glad of the distraction, had they crashed. It was her last chance this season to be selected for the team – something she craved. She wanted to be part of something, to prove what she was capable of.

Was she up to it?

As the journey unwound, Erin fantasised excuses. *I could cope with a broken leg,* she reasoned. Broken bones were part of being an equestrian. The best thing about being injured was watching TV all day and eating as much ice cream as you could stuff in your face. *Perhaps a flat tyre would do it.* The voice in her head cultivated seeds of doubt and it took all her strength to hold them at bay.

She'd never forgive herself if she didn't make it. It meant *everything.* It didn't matter how often Inés or Caoimhe told her it was no big deal – it *was* a big deal and nothing they could say would make her feel better if she failed again. They didn't get it. It was easy for them to say it didn't matter, that it was fine to fail. They didn't know what failure was. They weren't the ones in the spotlight. She absolutely could *not* fail again. She needed to qualify for the Spanish show. The British team selectors would be scouting there and there was no choice but to succeed. Her stomach churned.

Erin loved jumping and anything to do with horses. It was one of the few times in her life when she felt totally free. But since her dad had passed away, every show and competition left her living on her nerves. It was all right for Caoimhe. She didn't care if she lost her taekwondo matches – not that she ever did. It wasn't fair.

She glanced over at Inés, whose eyes were firmly on the road. An oppressive silence filled the cab. Inés wasn't as full of her usual attempts to keep Erin focused and optimistic. Although Erin preferred it this way, she was also astute enough to realise that Inés didn't seem herself. 'Are you okay, mum? Looking out for any rogue trees?'

Inés smiled, although she didn't take her eyes from the road as she manoeuvred the large truck expertly around the bends.

'Yes, darling,' she muttered. Then she said hurriedly, 'I saw an old friend at the de Bohuns' last night. Do you remember your Uncle Kent?'

'Dad's friend? He's not my uncle.'

Inés slowly tilted her head as if falling further into her line of thought, eyes still fixed ahead but her stare softening. 'Well, he is – was – a very close family friend.' Her words deliberate, Erin could almost see the cogs turning in her mother's head. When she was that careful about speaking, it meant lots was going on behind the scenes. Erin shrugged. She vaguely remembered him, but couldn't remember much about him other than he'd been smarmy and way too attentive to her mother. Dad had thought he was great.

'Yeah, I remember. So, he was there?' Erin wriggled uncomfortably. Something about Kent had always made her feel *icky*.

'Yeah, turns out he's done some work with Guy. It was nice to see him actually … we'd lost touch over the last couple of years. I was thinking I should invite him round for supper, maybe? I know he'd love to see you all.'

Inés' voice was almost too casual now. Erin made a movement similar to her last shrug. 'Whatever.'

'Well, we're here.' Inés abruptly turned into the car park. Erin was itching to get out and get warmed up, adrenalin running through her body.

'You're going to be fine,' Inés told her firmly, her voice more serious than that of her usual pre-show pick-me-ups. 'Absolutely fine. Imagine how great you're going to feel when you lift that cup up. Keep focused on that and don't get caught up in your head. You've got this, Erin.'

'Yeah. I've got this.'

The pair meandered through their pre-competition tasks. Inés was filling in for the groom again. After bringing out Baby's equipment, Erin packed her sports bag and checked the time and which arena they would be competing in. They were both lost in their thoughts.

As Erin started to get Million Dollar Baby ready, she saw Benjamin de Bohun walking towards her with a smirk on his face.

'Hi,' said Erin, flatly. Before he could respond, she turned to her phone and stared at it, hoping he'd take the hint. As long as she'd known Ben, he had been a thorn in her side. Most people's impression of Ben was that he was a Jack the Lad, boisterous and confident. He captained the rugby team at Chapter House and truly believed himself to be something special. But Erin knew him for what he was – a sly bully.

'Erin! I wanted to come and wish you good luck. You'll need it if last week was anything to go by.' His face cracked into a smile that didn't reach his eyes, goading her.

She resisted the urge to grind her boot into his toe, like she'd done before. He'd been teasing Caoimhe about her red hair and made her cry. Elizabeth had carried on as though Erin had tried to break her precious boy's leg. With the yelling coming from Ben and his mother, she wished she'd done more damage to make it worth it.

'You're too kind,' Erin said with mock sweetness. 'Tell me, did you hear back from Eton? Your mum told mine months ago you'd appeal their rejection – again.' She paused, then said with as much sweetness as she could muster, 'What happened?'

'I hope you ride your best out there today,' Ben said with fury. 'No matter how hard you try, it'll never be good enough. You know that, right? I don't want you to get your hopes up. You've reached your limit.' He paused. 'A shame, but it happens to all amateurs.'

Her gaze fell to the ground.

A group of adults was approaching, hot dogs in hand.

Ben said in a softer tone: 'It will be great to have you in Spain, if you can make it.' With that, he departed with a swagger.

Erin shrugged. *Sarcastic wanker.* As if anyone would be fooled by that friendly act.

Inés came back with some Cokes. They saw Guy at the other side of the show ring and waved at him. 'Elizabeth doesn't seem to be here this week,' Erin noted. That was one blessing at least.

Inés grinned. 'The amount she was putting away last night, I bet she cried off with a headache.' Her mother's chuckle made Erin laugh and she felt her anxiety lift. Then she noticed Inés' gaze following one of the show officials as he walked past. Erin looked at him, her cheeks flushing as she realised why he'd caught her mother's eye. He was tall and muscular, with dark hair that highlighted his perfect white teeth. *They couldn't be real, surely? No one has teeth that white.*

'He's very handsome,' Inés commented, flicking back her hair. The man noticed her and made a beeline for them.

'Good morning, young lady,' he said, although his attention was clearly on her mother. 'Erin, yes? And Million Dollar Baby. This is your last chance to qualify for Spain.'

Thanks for reminding me, Erin thought.

'She's going to qualify,' Inés said firmly, almost challenging the man to disagree. Erin saw admiration flicker in his eyes.

'I like that kind of confidence,' he said, flashing his teeth. He held a hand out to Inés. 'I'm Jack, by the way. Hopefully I'll see you again in Spain.'

'You can count on it,' Inés said, smiling. Jack walked off, though not before giving Inés another admiring look.

'That was *so* cringe,' Erin said, shaking her head.

'Nothing wrong with a little flirt,' Inés retorted.

'He's one of the team selectors,' Erin pointed out.

Inés simply nodded.

Ten minutes later, Erin's number was announced. She rode towards the ring, her thoughts focusing on the task in front of her. The voice in her head echoed Ben's words. *No.* She focused on her father instead. She remembered how he encouraged her before her first competition and each one thereafter. 'You can do it, princess,' he'd told her, his warm eyes twinkling. 'You just have to believe it. Now go smash it!' He'd always been her biggest champion. Erin hadn't realised how much confidence her father had given her until he was gone.

Since his passing, she tried not to think about him at a show, worried that would upset her too much and cause her to fail. But Ben's words had cut deep, today. She closed her eyes and the memory of her father's warmth filled her, replacing anxiety with faith. Filled with confidence and assurance, she felt him close to her. Her eyes opened and she saw his face in the crowd.

Erin took a deep breath. Million Dollar Baby was poised and electric beneath her, contained and powerful, blood pumping with anticipation.

They were off.

Erin felt her nerves drop away as Baby cantered towards the first jump, and a calm, single-pointed focus came over her. She collected him together and bang! They were in unison.

They flew over the first few jumps and Erin leaned into her horse, feeling his muscular strength underneath her, keeping her eyes firmly on where they needed to go. She supported him a little more this time and made him wait for the jump, rather than taking the corners too quickly.

Baby cleared it perfectly. In fact, the entire course was perfect, and Erin beamed from ear to ear as they trotted out of the ring. She held her breath for her time, catching Inés' eye. The look of pride in her mother's face was unmistakable.

She was going to Spain.

• • •

Back at the yard, she helped unload the horsebox. Erin loved it. Inés had bought this one two years ago, for 'a total bargain', but it still cost the same as a two-bedroomed house. Erin thought it was the most beautiful thing she'd ever seen. She daydreamed about living in it. Like a mobile home. Setting off around the world with her beloved ponies in the back and pitching up where she felt like.

Erin smiled as she placed Baby's rugs on his warm body. She smoothed them down with her hand and gently spoke to him. Although her anxiety would no doubt return once she was faced with the selection classes in Spain, she could, for now, relax. She'd done it – and in record time, too. She couldn't wait to tell Caoimhe.

Erin made her way to the house, excited to tell everyone the good news. Before she had time to open the front doors, Caoimhe swung them open, took one look at her sister's face and shrieked with delight. 'You did it!'

'Yep,' Erin said, aiming for nonchalance and failing. Caoimhe hugged her and then took a step back and looked at Inés, her forehead creasing.

'But won't Spain clash with me going to Sweden?' The taekwondo competition in Sweden for Caoimhe's age group started a few days after Erin's qualifiers.

Inés shook her head with a smile. 'You girls think I wouldn't have prepared for this? It's sorted. We'll go to Spain with Jane and then one of us will go with you to Sweden.'

Erin knew the 'one of us' would be Jane, because without the comforting, motivating presence of their mother, Erin would be a bag of nerves. She wished she could be more like her younger sister and not worry so much. Caoimhe never *seemed* to mind that Erin got that bit of extra attention, but she couldn't help wondering if her little sister was hiding resentment.

Caoimhe grinned. 'Sorry, mum. I should have known you're on the ball. Can I see if Charlie wants to come for dinner?'

'Why not?' Inés laughed. 'He usually does.' Caoimhe grabbed a bunch of keys and ran for the quad bike. She'd pick up Charlie, taking the long route so she could blaze around the fields as fast as she could.

'Are we all going?' Erin asked. Usually, Jane stayed at home with the younger girls, but they'd never had such important competitions at exactly the same time before.

Inés shook her head. 'Fiadh and Imogen have SATs. They're going to stay here with grandma. Lily will have to come. She'd be too much for granny on her own, what with her bad hips.'

What with her drinking, more like. Erin decided not to say anything as Alice was only in the next room. She went up to her bedroom to get changed, still feeling the fizz of victory. This part of competing made it worth it. She was walking on air.

Charlie came over for dinner wearing an unseasonably warm scarf and his hair sticking out from under his cap in all directions.

After dinner, Erin walked Charlie to the door, said goodbye with a huge hug and then squeezed his hand, depositing something private within. She whispered in his ear: 'I wish you'd talk to me or mum. Honestly, she always knows what to do.'

Charlie looked at her. 'It'll be fine. Don't worry about me. I'll deal with it.'

Erin gave him a doubtful look. 'If you say so.'

Charlie dropped his eyes and there was an awkward silence before he added, 'I am glad I have you as a friend, though.'

'Yeah,' Erin said, giving him a smile. 'Me too.'

Charlie hung there awkwardly, as if he wanted to say something else. But finally, he said, 'Well, bye, then.'

'See you tomorrow?'

'See you soon.' Charlie offered a bashful glance at her before meandering into the darkness.

Erin shut the door after him and turned to see Inés coming down the stairs. She gasped. 'Mum, you look great!'

A designer silver dress hung on her mother, the loose fabric – accentuating her tall slender figure – cut in a deceptively simple design. A plunge neck reached the base of her breastbone. Her large green eyes sparkled from behind dark, smudged eyeliner. Erin thought her mother looked like a movie star.

Inés looked unsure, standing awkwardly. 'Thank you, darling,' she said, 'but are you sure you don't mind me going out again? I mean, I was out last night.'

'Mum, you are allowed a life, you know. It's not like you do it all the time.'

It was good that her mother was going out and enjoying herself. Plus, Erin enjoyed the freedom she had with Inés out, grandma in her room nursing a bottle of whiskey and Jane in her annex next door.

Inés stepped off the bottom stair and gave Erin a hug, although she was careful not to crease her dress. The familiar smell of her mother's Chanel perfume wafted around them; it was rich and comforting, and brought back memories of her father. 'You're a pet. Don't wait up, okay? I'll be fine.'

As Inés left to get her cab, Erin wondered if she would ever be as glamorous as her mother or if she'd always feel this awkward and out of place.

Chapter Six

Inés sipped her champagne and peered over the balcony to the club below. Chris had promised it would be a great opening night, and he was right. The club was heaving and Inés was grateful for the relative calm of the VIP lounge.

The heavy bass from the music pounded through her feet, throbbing in time with the pulsing of the purple lights that lined the wall. On a podium in the corner, inside what looked like a gilded cage, danced a guy in skin-tight trousers and nothing else. Stunning waitresses walked around with drinks trays, clad in shimmering gold silk that clung to their lithe bodies in a way that was somehow demure and scandalous at the same time.

'So, what do you think?' Chris asked, bringing her back into the moment. It was just the two of them sitting on the plush leather sofa – Tabby had cried off with morning sickness that had lasted all day.

'I like it,' Inés said, glancing around. She saw a few famous faces; models and actors and some socialites. She was glad there were no trashy celebrities. That wasn't her scene at all.

She eyed the dancer in his cage, giggling when she

saw Chris doing the same. He was a free spirit, without inhibition, and judging from the number of eyes on him, everyone who met him seemed enthralled by him. He wore a tailored midnight blue suit, a slight heel on his boot, and had the most flawless dark brown skin.

'Does he bat for your side or mine do you think?' Chris purred, nodding at the caged man. Inés frowned as the dancer looked over and winked with a smile that seemed to encompass them both.

'Maybe he's keeping his options open?' she suggested.

'I'll let you have him,' Chris said airily. 'You could do with a one-night stand.'

Inés glared at him. 'It's not nice, making fun of a poor widow like that,' she said in a mocking tone.

Chris snorted unsympathetically. 'There's nothing poor about you, darling! And you've been a widow for four years. I'm beginning to think you should have stayed with Boring Bobby.'

'I did sort of see someone last night,' Inés confided and began to tell him about bumping into Kent. Raff briefly flashed into her mind but she pushed his image away. It would be terrible if she suddenly professed an interest because he'd turned out to be a lord. Yes, he was handsome, and more interesting than she'd ever given him credit for, but he was her girls' head teacher and seemed to have a girlfriend. Totally unsuitable. Not that she was interested.

'George's old business partner? The American?' he asked, eyebrows raised. 'We met at that barbecue you had for Caoimhe's birthday. He's absolutely gorgeous and definitely fancies you. He couldn't take his eyes off you.'

'He's always tried to look out for us. He was close to George—'

Chris waved his manicured hand, cutting her off. 'Darling, it wasn't a paternal look. He wanted you then and there, over that hot barbecue, so he wants you now. Go for it.'

When Inés hesitated instead of replying, Chris looked at her seriously. 'Is it because of George? Because they were friends?'

Inés nodded. 'I suppose so. It's not that it feels wrong exactly. George would have wanted me to get on with things – it's too close to home. Did I ever tell you that we'd been thinking of trying an open marriage?'

Chris rolled his eyes. 'Darling, it was me who suggested it. Though I didn't expect you to take it *that* seriously.' He placed a strong loving arm around her shoulder and pulled her closer.

'Yes, well, somehow I don't think he had his best friend in mind, do you? It feels … disloyal, somehow.'

Chris smiled sympathetically. 'Inés, we all miss him terribly and I know you want to do what's best for your family, but you're talking as though he's still alive. He's gone. You're single. Your oldest is sixteen. At this rate, you'll be a grandmother before you actually get laid again.'

Inés shook her head, not knowing whether to laugh or chide him. She sighed heavily, remembering her dark thoughts the previous night in the orangery. They'd continue to weigh on her mind if she didn't share them. She'd kept them hidden for so long.

'Chris,' she began hesitantly, 'Do you ever think that George's fall might have been – deliberate? I think he was in a financial mess. His business wasn't doing as well as he'd let on.'

'Was he, now?'

She nodded. 'Kent bought me out, otherwise I could have lost a lot. George didn't say a word to me while he was alive, so he must have been terrified about anyone finding out.'

Chris put down his glass slowly and stared at her for a long moment before he spoke. 'Inés, two things. One, there's absolutely no way George would have deliberately done that to you and the girls. Lily was only a baby! He doted on them. Two, how long have you been suspecting this, and why have you never told me? Honestly, I'm hurt.'

He pouted theatrically to take the edge off his words, but Inés knew he *was* hurt by her concealment of this. 'No, I only found out because I received a letter from the tax office a few days ago.'

'Does Tabby know?'

'No,' Inés reassured him firmly. 'I didn't tell anyone, as saying it out loud may have made it real. And I didn't want to speak ill of George.'

'But you've been carrying these thoughts around, even before you got the letter? Admit it.'

Inés nodded then knocked back the rest of her drink. Its warmth filled her stomach. *I don't want to be sad any more.* 'I thought I'd put it behind me, to be honest, but seeing Kent brought it back. I suppose that's another reason I'm wary of anything happening between us.'

'You should ask him.'

'About his intentions towards me?'

'About George's state of mind that night. If there was any indication – not that I believe it for a minute. Surely Kent would have picked up on it?'

A good point, Inés thought as she signalled a waitress over to top up her glass. But how on earth could she ask? It was hardly a conversation starter. Once Kent had bought her shares and George's half of the business, they'd never discussed it again.

The waitress shimmied over to top up their glasses, eyeing Chris curiously. She looked young and less than confident as she filled Chris' glass to the brim.

'Darling,' Chris asked her, leaning forward with a conspiratorial look, 'what's that delicious cage dancer called?'

'Lucas.'

'And what time does Lucas finish his performance?'

The girl glanced at the ornate clock hanging on the back wall. 'The dancers rotate. He'll be finishing soon and won't be back on until midnight. Do you want me to tell him you were asking about him?' A ring of Cockney circled through her voice.

'Oh yes,' Chris said with a smile. 'Do invite him over for drinks, won't you?'

'Chris!' Inés laughed, her worries momentarily forgotten. 'Stop using the poor girl as a go-between. I am sorry,' she added, addressing the young waitress who told her not to worry before she blushed and hurried away.

Inés tutted, but she envied Chris' confidence as much as she lamented her loss of it. She was fearless in every other way, but clueless with men – or at least the pursuit of men. Battling the male, pale and stale in the financial districts of Europe and the US was far less intimidating and confusing than dating.

She'd never had to worry with George. They'd met while still young after she'd had her wild university years, and he'd managed to turn her head long enough to slip a ring on her finger. She hadn't minded. He was a good match and her mother liked him. She'd done all the things a woman does: career, marriage, kids. She and George had been a great team and great friends. And that was it; simple.

'You're terrible,' she said. 'I take it that online dating isn't working for you at the minute?'

'I can't get on with it,' Chris said with a sigh. 'All that talking and messaging with someone only to meet up and find out they either look nothing like their picture or they're completely devoid of personality. And if you do end up sleeping with them, it's so boring and clinical. It's exhausting. Besides, I like catching someone on the spot. You can only feel chemistry when you're face-to-face. Life is too short for bad sex.'

'Probably not something I should try then.' Inés knew it wouldn't be her scene at all.

'Definitely not. You need something more upmarket.' Chris feigned an even stronger plummy accent.

'You're not calling me a snob again, are you?' Inés laughed. 'I forgot to tell you,' she went on, 'but you know Mr Taylor from the girls' school?'

'The handsome teacher? Yes. Oh please, tell me he's gay?'

'No,' Inés grinned. 'I bumped into him at the de Bohuns' soirée. Turns out Mr Taylor is in fact Lord Byron-Taylor.'

Chris' perfectly lined mouth fell open. 'He's nobility? Why on earth is he teaching in a school?'

Inés told Chris of their conversation, trying to keep the sudden pang of disappointment out of her voice when she mentioned Clarissa.

Chris had other ideas. 'There you go then, Inés. He's the perfect man for you. No reason why you shouldn't jump *his* upper-class bones. Shame about the lack of inheritance, of course.'

'There is absolutely a reason,' Inés said firmly. 'He's completely unsuitable.'

'More so than Kent?'

Inés opened her mouth to respond when she felt her phone vibrate. She opened the bag to see a familiar name on the screen. 'Speak of the devil,' she murmured. 'Kent just texted me.'

'Good, invite him along,' Chris suggested. 'Then you won't feel like a third wheel when Lucas comes over.'

'You're so sure of yourself!'

'Looks like we're about to find out.' Chris nodded over to the cage, where Lucas was stepping out to be replaced by a female dancer with long dreadlocks and a leopard print two- piece. The waitress who had served them went over to Lucas and said something to him, nodding her head towards Chris and Inés. Chris sat up straight and looked over at Lucas with his best smouldering look. Lucas headed straight over to their table.

'Told you,' Chris murmured before plastering on his most seductive smile.

Poor Lucas doesn't stand a chance, Inés thought.

It quickly became obvious that Lucas was more than happy to be seduced. Ten minutes later, he and Chris were flirting for England. Inés reached into her bag to read the message from Kent.

Where r u?

She guessed he was out too, perhaps at the tail-end of business drinks, or at one of the West End's better wine bars. Kent had expensive tastes.

At a club with Chris.

She was about to place her phone back in her bag when it vibrated again. Kent had answered her immediately. Inés felt a flip of pleasure in her stomach.

In Soho?

Yes.

Where?

Inés hesitated and then wondered why. It was Kent; they'd been out drinking together countless times in years gone by. *Although*, she reminded herself, *not without George.*

'Kent wants to join us, I think,' she said to Chris, tapping him on his shoulder to divert his attention from Lucas.

'Of course he does. Let him.'

'Who's Kent?' Lucas asked. 'Your partner?'

'No, no, definitely not,' Inés responded, flustered. 'A …
family friend. Nothing interesting at all.'

'When people say that, it usually means it's something
very interesting,' Lucas said over the music.

Inés ignored them and quickly, before she could talk
herself out of it, sent Kent the address of the club. 'Will he
be able to get in the VIP area?' she asked. The rest of the
club was heaving now, and she didn't fancy joining the
crush at all.

'Yes, you're with me,' Lucas said. 'Tell him to ask for
Lucas and I'll let the guy on the door know.'

Inés texted Kent while Lucas made his way to the VIP
entrance. Then she looked up at Chris, wanting confir-
mation she was doing the right thing. *It was just a drink.*

'Don't ask him lots of questions about George,' Chris
admonished. 'You need to let it go, especially on a night
out.'

Inés ignored him. 'So, what do you think of Lucas?'

'A bit young and arrogant,' Chris mused. 'Definitely not
marriage material.'

'Are you looking for a husband?'

Inés expected Chris to chuckle. Instead, he pulled a
face into his glass. 'I don't know, Inés, I'm not getting any
younger. Maybe settling down wouldn't be so bad.'

Inés thought that if he wanted to settle down, meeting
dancers in clubs probably wasn't the best way to go about
it, but decided not to voice her opinion. It was Saturday

night. They were supposed to be having fun. She was always so sensible, at work and with her family, she sometimes had to remind herself it was okay to relax and let go.

A track Inés recognised came on and she got up and moved into the small dance area – which was already full of people – and let her body move in time to the rhythm. She loved dancing, and she knew she moved well. Unaware of the admiring looks from a table of men in the corner, she lost herself in the music.

'You look divine.' A voice came from behind her, smooth, low and confident. It was Kent. She turned and smiled at him. In a crisp white shirt and tailored chinos, he looked younger than his years and undeniably handsome.

'Thank you. Do you want to sit down?' His arrival had sent a gentle shiver down her spine and she was thankful her voice didn't waver.

'Not yet,' he said, stepping towards her. 'I want to dance. With you.'

Kent started to match her rhythm, one hand lightly resting on her hip, and although there was nothing overtly sexual in his touch or movements, Inés was acutely aware of their closeness, the warmth of his hand through her dress and the throbbing in her body from the bass as the music travelled up from the club below. George had never danced with her like this. They moved naturally together, as they danced hip to hip, and she couldn't help but feel attracted to Kent's advances.

The music changed to a faster beat and Inés smiled ruefully, not sure whether she was disappointed or relieved. 'Let's go and say hi to Chris,' she said, leading Kent towards the couch.

Lucas and Chris were kissing.

'He looks kinda busy,' Kent commented drily.

'He does, rather. Shall we find a separate sofa?'

They made their way to an empty seat and sat down. Kent's knee was a millimetre from hers and she felt its heat. He leaned his upper body into her space. She wondered if he was going to try to kiss her and how she'd react if he did. She glanced at his mouth and then remembered what she wanted to ask him.

'Kent,' she said quietly, her tone serious, 'I need to ask you something. That letter – it brought those old fears back. I can't stop wondering again…'

He nodded, looking curious. 'Ask away.'

Inés hesitated, and then blurted: 'Do you think George might have – jumped? From the boat?'

Kent's eyes widened. He seemed lost for words – most unlike him – and Inés hurried to explain. 'It's just – he'd got himself into debt and never said a word. I know he'd have been terribly embarrassed and feel like he'd let us down. George was like that.' She paused, her stomach curling with dread as she waited for his reply.

Kent took her hand between his, his skin warm and smooth against her own. She caught a scent of expensive hand cream. 'Inés,' he said, gazing into her eyes like a lover, 'George would never have deliberately left you and the girls. I'm certain of it. Yes, he'd got himself into a mess and I don't doubt it affected him, but he wouldn't do that.'

'You're sure?' Inés realised she'd been holding her breath, her hand tightening, seeking his support. Kent nodded his head firmly and Inés exhaled with relief.

'I'm sure. He'd drunk more than usual, perhaps because of the pressure he must have been feeling, but that's all. It was an accident, Inés.' He shook his head. 'Have you been worrying about this the whole time?'

'I don't think I realised what I was thinking until recently,' Inés confessed, 'but yes, I suppose it was lurking in the back of my mind.'

Kent squeezed her hand. 'Is that why you haven't moved on?'

'I have moved on,' Inés protested. 'Everything has come together well, the yard is on the up, I've been promoted, the girls are thriving…'

'But you're still on your own.'

'I like being on my own,' Inés said defiantly. 'And I *have* dated … it's just never interested me that much. Or I haven't found anyone interesting enough. Besides, no one can keep up with me. I have high standards – and high stamina,' she said with a flirtatious laugh.

Kent smiled slowly. That look was back in his eyes, the one that made her body warm right to its core. 'Maybe now you've got that resolved, you'll be able to find someone who meets your standards.' He lifted his other hand and ran it lightly down Inés' cheek. 'You're a beautiful woman, Inés.'

'Thank you.' She held his gaze and then looked away demurely. She knew Kent was stirring. He dropped his hand, looking momentarily awkward. Inés looked over at Chris to see if he'd noticed, and then realised that he and Lucas had vanished.

'Well, it appears someone is going to have a good night,' she laughed.

'He moves fast, doesn't he? Would you like another drink?'

Inés thought about it. She could stay here with Kent and see where the night led them. It was tempting to throw caution to the wind and let him take her home. Tipsy Inés was saying yes, and it felt as though it had been a long time coming between them. A wild one-night stand could be just what she needed. But common sense won out, and she shook her head. 'I should get going,' she said. 'We're off to Spain soon and it's Erin's chance to be selected for the British team; it's a big moment for her. Plus, I have a lot of work to do this coming week before we go. I need a clear head. Perhaps when I get back?'

Kent looked disappointed, but smiled graciously. 'Of course, let's take a rain check. I'll walk you to a cab.'

They headed to the taxi rank, Kent's hand at home on the small of her back. Outside, the cold air hit her with a sting and Kent draped his jacket around her shoulders while she waited for a taxi. One pulled up and she turned her cheek to Kent before stepping inside. He took her chin gently in his hand, turning her face to his and brushing his lips softly against hers. Inés felt a jolt of electricity shoot through her as her body immediately responded.

'Are you sure you won't change your mind about that drink?' he asked.

Inés could see desire in his eyes. She smiled, enjoying the momentary sense of power. 'Goodnight, Kent. I'll call you from Spain,' she promised as she shut the taxi door.

Chapter Seven

Most mornings, Inés enjoyed the drive from her home into work. It only took an hour or so from the Surrey Hills – if she left home early enough – into the capital. But the contrast amused her; from the sprawling old Tudor house and stables set amidst some of the best scenery the English countryside had to offer, to the bustle and business of vibrant London. She thought the juxta-position captured her life quite well; from horse mum to CFO, responsible for managing the financial actions of the whole company and those it absorbed. Inés enjoyed her job, though more and more it felt as though she was attending training seminars rather than overseeing the finances of the company. It kept her mind keen; it was very difficult to get one over on her, with numbers anyway. She liked numbers, they made sense, especially compared to the disarray of teenage emotion and male intention.

Maybe that was why the tax bill had thrown her for a loop. She wasn't used to letting things like that go. And with the sale of the company – George's company – she hadn't thought she'd have to worry about it. It wasn't just the money – it felt like old demons, coming back to haunt her.

Inés drove to work, her eyes on the traffic but her mind elsewhere. They were heading to Spain soon and she was preparing herself for the usual antics among the horse mums. Inés was a support for her daughter, but some of the mums treated shows as an excuse for a knees-up; an escape from the entrapments of responsibility at home. Their need to get away usually took precedence over the show, and some of the Brits were an embarrassment – staying up all night drinking, being hung-over for classes and starting fights with locals.

She'd travelled extensively herself for work and plea-sure, and she'd tired of it. Business trips weren't nearly as glamorous as people thought. While the horse mums used any excuse to get away, Inés searched for excuses to stay at home.

Inés tried not to think about Kent, George or the letter, but they played on her mind, weighing on her as heavily as the swollen black clouds on the horizon. It would be raining before she got to London, she was sure. It always happened on the days she didn't bring her umbrella.

The tax letter must have been a mistake. She'd seen the books years ago and knew that this sum was definitely incorrect. But now she had to deal with contacting HM Revenue & Customs, which was a tedious endeavour at the best of times. And getting them to admit a mistake; that was nearly impossible. Inés resolved that this was a problem which needed all the ammunition she could obtain. Old documents would have to come out of storage and she'd have to approach Kent for anything he could give her that would help.

Spain. After Spain, I'll tackle this.

Just as she'd thought, the rain cloud burst and everything was enveloped in a sheet of grey. Fat raindrops bounced off her windscreen. Inés was grateful for the covered parking space that came with her job.

She was stuck in the usual London traffic and crawling along when Chris phoned. 'Aren't you at work?'

'Just got into the office. First one in. Darling, I saw Lucas again yesterday. He's divine, and I think this one may last a while.'

'Really?' Inés grinned. She'd be delighted to see Chris find someone who truly appreciated him.

'Well, we'll see, I don't want to jump the gun … but we do get on *very* well.'

'Spare me the details,' Inés laughed, although she knew she'd be pumping him for information the next time they went out for drinks together.

'The thing is,' Chris continued, 'he's working at some club this weekend that I don't like the sound of – too down market for my tastes. So, I'm at a loose end. Didn't you say a while ago that the Hunt Ball was on?'

'I did,' Inés confirmed, 'but I've no plans to go – I fly out to Spain on Monday.'

'That's plenty of time to recover! You're getting old.' Chris tutted. 'That sort of thing would never have stopped you before. Let's go, darling. They're such fun and I don't want to be sitting around all weekend fretting over what Lucas is doing.'

He really is smitten, Inés thought. 'I'll think about it,' she promised. 'I suppose it couldn't hurt to go for a few hours. I'm not staying for breakfast though; these things can get wild, you know that.'

The Hunt Balls were thought of by most as stuffy old affairs for those not wanting to let go of the glory days of fox hunting. In truth, they were an excuse for a lively all-nighter. Some were known for including a breakfast at 5am before carriages at 6:30am. It was funny to see the geriatrics, usually so well presented, on the dance floor and doing the *walk of shame* in the early hours.

'Of course, it's why I like them,' Chris said promptly. 'Better go. The manager is coming in. Speak later, darling.'

'Bye,' Inés trilled, but he'd already rung off. Chris never failed to lift her spirits.

She walked into her office and smiled at the cleaner who was exiting. She was a little early, which she liked and was expected of her in such a senior position. Hanging up her coat and firing up her computer, she checked her diary for the day. Busy as ever, but thankfully no meetings, which meant she could more or less prioritise her own work and, if she managed to get ahead this morning, she'd have time for a quick lunch at the French cafe across the road, which had the best coffee Inés had ever tasted.

She was just getting started when her colleague, Mark, popped his head around the door.

'Morning, Inés. I'm going to fetch a coffee from the kitchen. Would you like one?'

'I'll have an espresso, please,' Inés replied, giving him a quick smile without tearing her eyes away from the computer. Inés was Mark's immediate superior, and she put his attentiveness down to this fact. Although he'd never dream of saying anything, Inés sometimes got the impression that he resented working for a woman. It wasn't anything she could put her finger on, but Inés hadn't made it this far without being able to pick up on such undercurrents. She watched him as he shut the door, flicking her eyes up when he'd turned his back. A few years younger than her, he was also handsome and a hit with the women in the office. He'd started at CCM a few years ago and had subtly tried to flirt with Inés on a few occasions, which she'd immediately – although politely – brushed off. Maybe that was why he resented her so much. Still, she mustn't be uncharitable. Mark was a hard worker and usually great company at work lunches, and most of the time an asset to have around. You couldn't get on with everyone at work and so her secondary thoughts of him fell away as quickly as they'd come.

I seem to be second-guessing everything at the moment.

Mark brought her coffee, throwing her a winning smile, and Inés accepted it gratefully. Breakfast had been a rushed affair that morning. Mark gave her a wave and left her to it, as Inés buried herself in work. At lunchtime she emerged from her office and was heading downstairs when she heard Mark call her. She turned around to see him jogging to catch up.

'Hey, Inés,' he said, catching up with her on the stairs. 'Are you going out for lunch? I'll join you. I need to get out of the office, I'm sure the air conditioning is playing up again. It's stuffy as hell.'

Inés shrugged amicably. 'Sure, why not? I was going to head over to Le Petit Café, over the road.'

'Sounds good, I haven't tried it.'

'Oh, you must, it's lovely.'

They walked across together, Mark chatting about his weekend while Inés half listened. He was complaining about his latest girlfriend, who it seemed was determined to spend him into the ground.

'Why on earth,' Inés asked as they sat down at a table near the window and waited for the waitress to take their order, 'would you let her loose with your credit card?'

Mark looked embarrassed and Inés felt sorry for him, realising that he was eager to impress, obviously as much in his personal life as he was at work.

'I suppose I wanted to make her feel special – and probably show off a bit,' he admitted. 'But now I'm starting to wonder if she's a gold digger.'

'It happens,' Inés sighed. 'And with both sexes. You need to put your foot down. You work hard for what you earn; don't let it be frittered away. If she cares about you, she won't care about having access to your credit card.'

'You're right,' Mark sighed, 'and it wouldn't be as much of a problem if I hadn't just been landed with a huge tax bill. I do some consultancy work on the side but judging by the size of this bill it doesn't seem to be benefiting me much.'

'Hmm,' Inés said thoughtfully. 'I'd double check with them that they haven't made a mistake. I just received an odd letter from the tax office myself.'

'Oh? Your girls ride, don't they? Is it anything to do with that?'

'No,' Inés said, bemused, 'it's related to my late husband's company, which I was an investor in. They claim I owe them a substantial amount of money, which makes no sense. My accountant is looking into it. It has to be a mistake. But now you've said that, I wonder if there's a glitch in the system this year? I'm sure it wouldn't be the first time.'

Mark nodded, looking cheered. 'I hope so; I'll phone them. Thanks, Inés, you always make me feel better. You're my role model.'

'I'm glad,' Inés said, smiling and wondering if she'd misjudged him after all. Though she thought his blatant attempt at arse-kissing was a little much.

They had a pleasant lunch – Inés paid for it as a treat – moving off the subject of money, and then it was back to work. Towards the end of the day, Inés was pulled in for an informal meeting with the managing director and their international relations officer. There was an urgent opening in their American department, and the director, William, wanted Inés' opinion. Inés was pleased. William was notoriously hard to impress and was considered something of a tyrant by his employees, but Inés had a lot of respect for him and knew he was impressed by her hard work and sometimes bullish mindset.

'He's only happy when he's unhappy,' his secretary told everyone who'd listen. William was permanently seething, ready to blow at the slightest provocation, like a pressure cooker left on the stove for too long. It didn't help that he wore his tie so tightly around his thick neck that it made his head look as if it was emerging from a noose, squeezed like a tube of toothpaste and flaring red, giving the illusion that the top of his face was wider than the bottom.

'My first thought,' Inés said, 'would be Mark. He's hungry for promotion, and very talented. Whether he's in a position to move abroad at short notice though, I've no idea.'

William looked unsure. 'He's good, but I don't know if he's there yet. This is a delicate situation. We need someone who can whip the US team into shape. It's a shame we can't spare you, Inés.'

Inés smiled cautiously. As flattered as she was, she didn't want to move abroad, mainly because of the children, though she couldn't let William know that. There were a lot of bosses who wouldn't place women in high-powered roles for that reason, and although she trusted William, that excuse wouldn't fly with him or anyone else in his position. 'Thank you for saying so, but I agree, I'm more valuable to the company here than across the pond.'

William nodded. 'You're right, as usual,' he said firmly.

As Inés drove home, she wondered what it would be like to pack up and leave for a few months or longer. She'd always fancied America, but the girls were happy here. And George's presence was still in every corner of their house. How could she leave that behind?

On that thought, she made a call confirming her and Chris' attendance at the Hunt Ball. She thought she should invite Kent along as she'd blown him out the last time she'd seen him, and was feeling guilty about it, but thought better of it. *Besides*, she thought, remembering the arousing but unsettling feeling of Kent's hands on her body as they had danced, *there is nothing wrong with playing hard to get.*

Inés was stuck in slow-moving traffic when her phone rang and she saw it was from the twins' class teacher, Miss Phipps. Frowning, she answered, wondering what the call was about. Of all her girls, Fiadh and Imogen were the least likely to prompt a call home. *Perhaps they'd done something outstanding*, she thought proudly.

'Hello?' Inés said gaily.

Miss Phipps sounded less than happy. 'Mrs Cullen? I hope I haven't caught you at work?'

'I'm on my way home. Is there a problem?' Suddenly, she felt worried, wondering if something had happened to them; perhaps Jane hadn't arrived to collect them? But no, they'd have phoned her straight away if that was the case.

'Well, I did let your nanny know about the situation earlier, but I was finishing clearing up the atrocious mess.

It's gone five in the evening and I still haven't left the class-room yet, so I thought I would give you a call myself. The twins didn't seem to take the situation seriously.'

'What situation?' Inés asked, bemused.

'Everyone in the class was asked to bring in something from home – some kind of object – that meant something to them – and give a ten-minute presentation on it.' Miss Phipps sounded distinctly annoyed, and Inés wondered what object the twins could have thought to take in that could have offended her so badly.

'Yes?' *Get to the point...*

'The girls decided to bring in Luther, their hamster.'

Inés bit her lip and tried not to laugh. And still failed to see why something this small had caused such unrest in their teacher. *She was in serious need of a sense of humour,* Inés had thought on more than one occasion.

'I see. Well, all I can say is I'm sorry and shall talk to them about it. I'm sure there's no harm done, though?'

'On the contrary,' Miss Phipps sniffed. 'The thing got loose and the children absolutely tore up the classroom looking for it. Hence why it's taken so long to tidy away. Josie Smythe-Weston has an allergy and I've had a formal complaint from her mother, and two of the boys got into a fight about who'd found the hamster behind the book-shelf. It's been absolute chaos.'

Inés pressed a hand to her mouth. 'I am very sorry,' she assured her, 'and I'll have words with the girls as soon as I get home. It won't happen again.' She sighed. Never a dull moment.

Chapter Eight

There it is. I heard it again!

Alice sat bolt upright in bed, her heart pounding as she listened intently to the noise that had once again woken her. Footsteps, and then the back door of the porch banging. Someone was leaving the house in the early hours of the morning or coming in – which meant someone had been or was currently inside.

She swung her legs over the side of her bed and reached for her dressing gown, cursing the fact that her old body wouldn't move as quickly as she needed it to. It hadn't always been that way; she'd toured Ireland in her youth with her traditional dancing, and her nimble legs had caught the eye of Inés' father. *If I tried to dance now,* she thought with a sigh, *people would put money on whether my back, hips or knees would go first.*

By the time Alice got to the back door, there was nothing to see. The door was locked as it should be, and Spanky sat by the entrance to the kitchen, wagging his tail when he saw her. She patted his head, looking into his eyes as though she could find a clue there.

She wasn't crazy. She knew her granddaughters thought she was barking mad and that Inés was worrying about dementia, too much alcohol, or a combination, but Alice's senses were still sharp and she knew what she was hearing. Someone – or something – was in the Cullen household at night who shouldn't be.

'But if that's the case,' she said out loud to Spanky, 'Why aren't you barking?'

Spanky thumped his tail on the floor.

'Silly mutt,' Alice said affectionately. She gave him a final pat and then turned around to return to her room. Then she screamed as she saw a figure at the top of the back stairs. Spanky jumped to his feet at the noise and gave an excited bark.

'Granny, it's me!' Caoimhe said.

Alice took a deep breath and composed herself. 'Why are you prowling around the house, young lady?'

Caoimhe looked offended. 'I'm hardly prowling, granny. I was going to the toilet. I have to be up in an hour for school anyway.'

'Right, well go back to bed, then,' Alice said. The fright had put her on edge. There wasn't much she could do against a burglar or a spirit from the afterlife, *but I'd have a bloody good go*, she thought before making her way back to her room. It was only when she was lying back in bed that she allowed herself a sigh of relief. The strange noises were making her jumpy, and it was so frustrating no one else heard them. Inés, Lily and Erin slept at the front of the large Tudor house, but the middle girls were at this end and were adamant that they never heard a thing. *Their mother's influence has knocked the sight out of them.*

Only one conclusion made sense. Whatever she was hearing, it was not of this world. Back at home, the existence of the other world was taken much more seriously. Everyone knew that spirits that hadn't been laid to rest would stalk the shadows, marshes and forests. Any time she tried to suggest that to her daughter, Inés looked at her as though she was losing her marbles.

She's such a bone-headed woman, Alice thought with a disdainful sniff. *She's completely forgotten her roots.*

Over breakfast, Alice didn't say a word. She'd had enough of being spoken to as though she was a silly old woman. Caoimhe, however, the little bugger, told them for her. 'Granny was hearing things again last night,' she announced as she reached for her fifth piece of toast.

Inés' eyes flickered to her mother. 'Did you?'

'Yes,' Alice said defiantly. 'Yes, I did. It sounded like someone running through the house and going out the back door. Then I saw Caoimhe wandering around.'

Inés looked sharply at Caoimhe. 'Were you up to anything, Caoimhe? I had enough yesterday with the twins' antics.'

'Miss Phipps said we could take in anything we wanted,' Fiadh and Imogen said simultaneously in sulky tones.

Well, they had her there, Inés thought.

'No, I wasn't,' Caoimhe said indignantly. 'I was going to the toilet and I heard granny talking to Spanky. Then she got scared and screamed.'

'You crept up on me,' Alice accused.

Inés sighed heavily. 'We haven't got time for this. I have a lot to do before the Spain trip. Go and get dressed. We'll talk later, mum.'

Alice knew what the talk would be like. Inés would ask her if she was feeling all right, and whether she'd been drinking before bed, and suggest a doctor's appointment. Alice wondered at what point her daughter had started taking care of her instead of the other way around. Old age had crept up on her before she was ready.

'Don't get old.' She leaned into Lily pushing her nose into the youngster's squishy face with a smile. 'Everyone treats you like you're a child again. Yes, yes they dooo,' she cooed.

Once Inés and the girls had left and Jane had taken the younger girls to school, Alice phoned her friend Rose for advice. She'd met Rose at her Tuesday night poker club, where they seemed to have been winning the same fifty pounds back from each other for the past year or so.

'I heard it again, Rose,' she confided. 'And the back door was locked and the dog was sitting right by it as though nothing had happened. Caoimhe was awake and she didn't hear a thing. I'm telling you, something's going on. There's a spirit in this house. Maybe even my son-in-law – there were no problems before he died. It's only been the past year or so.'

'It could be,' Rose agreed.

At least she understands, Alice thought. Rose originated from the Welsh valleys, and she too had grown up taking it for granted that there were things the rest of the world didn't understand. 'You need a priest, Alice. That's the only thing that can sort this out. Or I could come and do a cleanse. Perhaps speak to the spirit and ask it what its unfinished business is?'

'I don't know,' Alice said, uncertain. She'd never had much use for priests. *More trouble than they're worth. Though a priest would be harder for Inés to argue with than my friends.*

A strong gust of wind through the open window behind her knocked an ornament from the shelf, making her jump. Then the wind was gone, as though it had come from nowhere.

'Have you got a number?' Alice asked.

Chapter Nine

'Well, they've certainly outdone themselves this year,' Chris said, sounding impressed as he looked around at the decor and then down at the menu. The Stanhope Hotel, an impressive country manor, had been built in the seventeenth century and had acted as host to an impressive supply of guests over the years, from royalty in bygone times to celebrities today. *Raff would look completely at home here,* Inés thought, letting her mind linger on Raff for the briefest of moments.

'They always do,' Inés replied. The Surrey and Berkshire Bloodhound Ball was renowned for putting on a good show, including a disco with all-night dancing, and despite the list of rules regarding how riders and guests were supposed to behave, Inés couldn't remember a year that she'd attended when those rules hadn't been broken at least once during the course of the night.

'Do you remember that time when the hunt went past, and the quarry was naked?' Chris asked, laughing. 'Did they get kicked out for that stunt?'

'Not that I know of,' Inés said, giggling as she remembered the group of attendees dressed in hunt regalia on the top and stockings and suspenders on the bottom, blowing horns and chasing the poor man through the main hall while the Macarena blared.

With the outlawing of fox hunting, the 'quarry' was no longer an animal, but a man – sometimes up to three men. While some manhunts smeared the quarry with animal blood, this was a 'clean boot' hunt, where the bloodhounds were trained to hunt a special man-made scent. It made for a great day out, and their annual balls were legendary.

Groups of circular tables were spread throughout the large room. White tablecloths, with posies of spring flowers in rustic pots clustered the centre of each.

'We're not going home too early, are we?' Chris pleaded, his head cocked endearingly to one side as they leaned against the bar, waiting for dinner to be served. The couple received admiring glances from some of the guests. Inés was dressed in a long, black shift dress and although she was in pain from having a horse stand on her foot a few days earlier, she'd still insisted on wearing strappy Jimmy Choo shoes. Chris looked as debonair as usual – in a fitted midnight blue suit with an open collar.

'Stop it,' Inés grinned. 'You know I need to get back at a decent time. We're off the day after tomorrow, and I have way too much to organise.'

'Oh, stop for a moment, will you, Inés? You'll be fine, darling,' Chris reassured her. 'You're one of the most organised people I know.'

'I have to be,' Inés sighed. 'I often feel like we're bordering on the edge of chaos, and I'm holding everything together with good intentions and a robust drinks cabinet.'

'It's not like you to feel like that. What's wrong? You're not still worried about George, are you?'

'No, not so much since I spoke to Kent. Getting the letter pulled me back to the past. Sometimes I wish I could have a little freedom and a break. Then I feel guilty for thinking like that.'

'Well, I think you're doing an amazing job.' Chris dropped a friendly kiss on the top of her head. 'And I love the near-chaos of your house, it's great fun. Better than being in my apartment on my own.'

'You know you're welcome any time,' Inés assured Chris. She felt that his jokes about being lonely were peppered with truth. 'It's easier when you're there. The girls love you so much. But my mum most of all. If she had her way, we'd be married – you do entertain her and give me a break when you visit.'

Chris smiled. 'She has great taste –'

'Oh,' Inés cut in. 'Talking of chaos, I forgot to tell you about the hamster.' She told Chris about Miss Phipps' phone call a few days before, and he laughed so loudly that the guests opposite them looked over in amusement.

Chris flashed them a winning smile. 'How's your mother doing?'

Inés was about to fill Chris in on her mother's latest run-in with the invisible intruder, when she felt her phone vibrate against her thigh. She frowned when she saw it was William, her boss.

'It's not like him to call on a weekend,' she said. 'There must be a problem.'

Excusing herself, Inés went outside to answer the call. 'William, I'm at a party. I hope everything is okay?'

William cleared his throat, a sound Inés knew from experience rarely heralded good news. 'I apologise for interrupting you,' he said stiffly. 'I would have waited until Monday to speak to you about this, but of course you're off to Spain.'

'What is it?' Inés asked, oddly nervous.

'I hope you know,' he said in a way Inés thought was likely meant to sound supportive, but came off as patronising nonetheless, 'that if you had any – personal problems, shall we say – you can come to me with them, and I'll do my best to help. You're a valued employee.'

Inés felt her stomach churn. *What now?* 'Of course. But, personal problems? I don't know what you mean.'

William exhaled heavily. 'I'm sure you can appreciate, Inés,' he said hesitantly, 'that as our CFO, you're expected to uphold a certain professional reputation. This carries over to your personal life. We're under the microscope of the law and the judgement of our clients and investors. Your financial integrity is important. You're very much the face of us.'

Inés felt a sour taste in her mouth as she understood there was only one thing William could be referring to. 'It's the tax letter I received, isn't it?' she demanded, swallowing her fury. 'Mark told you.'

'He was concerned, as I was when he mentioned it to me. Mark said he'd got the impression it was weighing on you heavily, and so I wanted to make sure there wasn't anything more going on here than some outstanding tax.'

Inés pressed the back of her hand to her mouth, feeling outraged at the deliberate act of sabotage. She'd been hoping to deal with this when she got back from Spain.

'No. It was simply and exactly that; outstanding tax on my husband's old company, which I no longer have anything to do with. My accountant is dealing with it, and I'm almost certain it's simply a mistake on the part of the tax office. If Mark has made out any more than that, he's lying.' Inés fought not to let the anger show in her voice, glad she hadn't confided in Mark any further. She'd never trusted him, but it hadn't occurred to her that he'd attempt such a deliberate act of troublemaking.

'That's a serious allegation,' William said.

'It's no more serious,' Inés snapped, 'than a junior colleague of mine coming to you with completely irrelevant information, trying to plant seeds of distrust about my professional and personal integrity. Honestly, William, I'm offended you've even entertained this.'

There was a pause, and Inés wondered if she'd been a little too honest, but when William replied she thought she detected a touch of contrition in his tone. 'I certainly didn't mean to offend you, Inés. Mark seemed genuinely worried, and I think he thought he was doing the right thing.'

'Right,' Inés said flatly. 'Well, I've thought for a while that he resents my position. I get the impression that he doesn't like working for a woman. In which case, his actions are completely nefarious.'

William went quiet again. Inés knew he'd think twice

before risking having his company associated with any type of sexism. 'I appreciate you giving me your side of things,' he told her, finally. 'I'll speak to Mark. Sorry to have interrupted you. Enjoy your night.'

'Thank you,' Inés said politely before walking back into the ballroom, seething. Chris raised an eyebrow as she approached.

'What's wrong?' he asked. Inés told him, and Chris gasped in disbelief. 'What an utter shit,' he said loudly.

'You can say that again. And just as I thought we were getting on better. I don't know how I'm expected to work with him now. It's as well I'm not in for two weeks, because I don't think I could stomach the sight of him.'

'I don't blame you. But don't worry,' Chris said sagely. 'I'm sure when William thinks about it, he'll see straight through Mark.'

Inés murmured in agreement, but the call had unsettled her more than she cared to admit. So far, it was no more than an exaggeration on Mark's part. There was no reason to think there was any problem beyond a simple mix up at the tax office.

But what if I'm wrong?

'Anyway, you'd be proud of me,' Inés continued. 'I managed to stop short of calling the snake a complete bastard to the boss.'

• • •

The following day, Inés had managed to put the letter to the back of her mind, and though she was still seething about Mark, she had the next two weeks to distract her. Luckily for him, she wouldn't have to talk to him while away. She had enough on her mind right now, including making sure Alice and the twins would be all right while she was gone. It would be as much a case of Fiadh and Imogen looking after granny as it would her mother looking after them. Resigning control to others – no matter how capable and trustworthy – was hard as she was such a perfectionist.

As though her thoughts had been read by her mother, Alice walked into Inés' bedroom. 'Something needs to be done, Inés.'

Inés looked up from where she was crouching on the floor. Her mother's grey hair was up in a cast-iron bun that sat askew with a few wisps of platinum white framing her thin face. She had a look of determination on her face.

Inés held back a sigh. 'About what, mum?'

Alice sat down heavily on the edge of the bed, crumpling the organic cotton sheets. 'The intruder. I know you think I'm making it up, but I heard them again early this morning.'

'I don't think you're making it up,' Inés answered patiently, 'but I do think you might be mistaken. It's probably one of the girls going to the toilet or Spanky trotting around downstairs. Think about it, mum. Spanky would bark the house down if there was a burglar.'

For a moment Alice looked as though she was about to agree with her, but then she shook her head resolutely, her mouth pursed, emphasising the wrinkles around her lips. It was as if Inés' words had confirmed something for her. 'No, I know what I'm hearing. Someone is in the house. In fact, I think I know who it is. And it would explain why Spanky isn't barking and no one else ever sees him.' Alice looked triumphant.

'Go on,' Inés said cautiously, wondering what theory her mother had come up with.

'It's George.'

Inés' eyes widened as she realised that Alice may have the onset of dementia. 'Mum,' she said, worry in her voice, 'George is dead. He died four years ago, remember?'

Alice glared at her, the same look she used to give Inés and her older brother Andrew when they'd been caught doing something forbidden as kids. Inés felt eight years old.

'Listen, young lady, I haven't lost my marbles yet. I'm talking about George's spirit. Maybe he's not at peace. I've always had a touch of the sight you know. Back home, it was a respected gift, at least in those days.'

Inés wasn't the type of person to believe in the old Irish tales of ghosts, banshees and the rest of it – but in light of the feelings she'd been having about George recently, the suggestion that he wasn't laid to rest was unnerving. *What if Kent were wrong?*

'Don't be silly, mum,' Inés said briskly. She stood up, changing the subject abruptly. 'Right, that's the girls' clothes packed, at least.' Then a thought occurred to her. 'You haven't said anything to the girls about this theory of yours, I hope?'

Alice tutted and looked offended. 'Of course I haven't. What do you take me for? Now, do you need a hand with anything?'

'Sorry,' Inés said, wanting to change the subject. 'Do you want to help me pack?'

'With my arthritis?' Alice sniffed. 'No, I'm going to watch TV.' She wandered off, leaving Inés staring after her, shaking her head in exasperation.

The doorbell rang and she got to her feet, wondering who it was likely to be at mid-morning on a Monday. She went downstairs and opened the door to see a huge bunch of flowers on legs.

'Erm, hello?'

The flowers were thrust into her hands, revealing a delivery man. 'For you. Special delivery.'

'Thank you,' Inés replied, bemused. She carried the heavy bouquet into the kitchen and set it down on the huge marble island. White orchids, white roses and saffron crocuses were expertly arranged on a bed of lilac ferns, and the scent immediately infused the whole kitchen. Inés reached into the middle of the bouquet for the gold-coloured card.

To the most beautiful woman I know.
Forget the drink. Let me take you for dinner.
I'll wait for your call.
Kent.

Inés set the card down on the table, her tummy fizzing. She was beginning to suspect that Kent wanted a lot more from her than a one-night stand.

Alice entered the kitchen, sniffing loudly. 'What's that smell?' Her eyes fell on the flowers and narrowed. 'Where have they come from?'

'Kent,' Inés said, gently stroking an orchid petal.

'Kent, George's friend? That Kent?'

'Yes, mum.'

Alice tipped her head to one side, still staring at the flowers. 'He likes you,' she announced, as though Inés hadn't yet worked that out.

'He wants to take me for dinner.'

'He wants a lot more than dinner,' Alice said. 'Men don't send flowers like that unless they're feeling guilty or they want to get you into bed, you mark my words. I've been around long enough.'

Inés grinned. 'Well, that's true. But I don't want a rundown of your youthful exploits, mum.'

'Don't be silly,' Alice tutted. 'I was a virgin when I met your father. You had to be in those days, especially in Ireland. But when I was a young widow … now those were the days.'

Inés grimaced and held up a hand. 'Mum, please,' she said. 'Let's get these in a vase and some water, shall we?'

'Maybe this is why George is still wandering around on the wrong side,' Alice said nonchalantly.

Inés gave her a horrified look, but her mother had already gone off to fetch the vase.

Chapter Ten

Later, with everything packed and ready to go to the airport, Inés made her way to the school to collect Lily. She wondered if she'd see Raff, and then tutted at herself for being concerned. Raff wasn't her type, blue blood or otherwise, and of course there was Clarissa.

Inés tried to ignore the fact that she was running out of reasons as to why Raff wasn't her type. Everyone seemed to like him and he was certainly handsome, although in a quieter, less flashy way than Kent.

Kent.

Inés thought back to the flowers that now graced her kitchen table, and the invitation that had come with them. Did she want to go out for dinner with him? It was becoming increasingly obvious there was chemistry between them. Her face grew hot as she remembered dancing with him, the smooth roll of his hips and the knowing look in his eyes. *He'd be great in bed.* She was sure of it.

She wondered if she'd offended him by turning down his offer of a drink – and the unspoken offer of more. But if she had, he was definitely not right for her. She could never be with a guy with such a fragile ego. And Kent wasn't used to being told 'no'. It would only make him chase her more. *It might be nice to be chased,* she mused.

As she pulled up outside the school, Inés checked her appearance in the rear-view mirror. Her hair was up in a scarf to protect it on the journey to come and she was wearing her comfortable sports luxe trousers and vest with an oversized open-zip sweater. She added a slick of lip gloss and expensive rouge. *Just because Raff isn't my type, doesn't mean I shouldn't make an effort*, she thought as she got out of the car, ignoring Chris' snide comments running around her head. Chris had phoned her that afternoon, still feeling the effects of his hangover, but also bubbling with excitement about Lucas. It seemed the dancer had barely left Chris' side, and he was already talking about him being 'the one'.

Inés walked over to the school entrance to wait for Lily, trying to ignore the disappointment she felt when she saw one of the class teachers in the doorway. Not in the mood for small talk with the other mums, she pulled out her phone, idly checking the hashtag for the upcoming qualifiers in Spain. She was part of an online group of horse mums, although she rarely posted anything, but now and then she wanted to catch up with the gossip. Right now, she wanted a heads up of who she could expect to see on the trip. The first post elicited an audible sigh from Inés. Maria Inglefield would be there, with her annoying daughter, Chelsea.

Chelsea's riding skills were hit or miss, and Inés hadn't expected her to make Spain; not that she begrudged the girl her progress, but the thought of spending two weeks in Spain with her mother dampened Inés' enthusiasm for going.

Maria was what Chris would call a 'superbitch'. Rich, beautiful, spoiled and unbearably narcissistic, she'd never seemed to like Inés. 'It's because you don't kiss her arse in the way she's accustomed,' Chris had told her, and Inés suspected he was right. Maria was an 'it girl', a former supermodel and daughter of a famous Hollywood actress and a British banking tycoon. She was now married to a wealthy property developer and her only job seemed to be posting heavily filtered pictures on social media, with the word 'Wonderlust' splashed everywhere – whatever that meant.

She called herself an 'influencer' and Inés had heard gossip of a recipe brand she was planning on releasing soon. She thought this was ironic as Maria had a private chef who went everywhere with her as part of her entourage. She'd probably never cooked a meal in her life.

Perhaps this trip was going to be interesting in more ways than one, Inés thought, an amused smile playing on her freshly glossed lips. Maria was in England because 'it's the only place to send your children to school,' or so she'd told a group of her Hollywood friends and Inés at one of her London parties last year. Inés cringed at the memory. She was convinced Maria thought it set her apart from her American friends and gave her some kind of status.

'Mummy!' Lily barrelled out of the doors and into Inés'

arms. Her ribbons had come loose and her knees were dirty, as usual. Inés laughed with exasperation. They'd have to watch her closely in Spain; Lily had a tendency to wander off and had absolutely no fear of anything.

'Are we going straight to the airport?' Lily asked, bouncing from one foot to the other with excitement.

'Not quite,' Inés smiled. 'We'll go home and wait for the others to get back, say goodbye to the twins and granny –'

'– and Spanky!'

'And Spanky, and then we'll be going as soon as we've had something to eat. Nanny Jane was making sandwiches when I left.'

Lily pouted. 'Sandwiches are boring. Can we bring Luther?' she asked.

Inés shook her head with a smile. 'Sorry, sweetheart, he doesn't have a passport.' She took Lily's hand and headed back to the car.

As she did, a deep and mellow voice said quietly: 'Airport? Are you off to Spain then?'

It was Raff, looking as crumpled as ever in his teacher's shirt and tie, running a hand through his floppy hair. *Lord Byron-Taylor.* Somehow, now she knew, she was amazed that she'd never suspected his background. Those cut-glass vowels, the aristocratic bone structure and the quiet, self-effacing yet still somehow utterly assured air he had.

'Yes, I told you about Erin's qualifiers? I did put a holiday request in.'

Raff chuckled. 'I wasn't questioning the timing. We'll miss you, that's all.'

His eyes locked on to hers and Inés felt suddenly flustered. 'You will?'

'Of course,' Raff beamed at Lily. 'She's quite the character. The school won't be the same with you gone.'

Inés wasn't sure why she felt deflated. 'Yes, right,' she said, feeling her cheeks flush.

'It was nice to see you at Elizabeth and Guy's the other night,' he went on, seemingly unaware of her embarrassment.

Inés nodded. 'Yes, you too. Not to mention a surprise. Clarissa seems nice,' she added, although she hadn't been impressed with the girl at all.

Jealousy?

'Er, yes.' Raff looked uncomfortable. 'She's a lovely girl I'm sure, though I don't know her well.'

'Oh, you don't? I assumed she was your partner. I do apologise,' Inés said feeling a surge of pleasure rush through her. Only because she'd got the impression that Raff and Clarissa weren't a particularly good fit, she told herself.

'No … it was our third date. Between you and me,' Raff lowered his voice, 'I doubt there'll be a fourth. How about you? I'm sure you must have plenty of men queuing up to take you out.'

Was he flirting with her? His tone hadn't changed, but there was an intensity in her eyes and she felt her stomach give another little flip.

Inés opened her mouth to reply, when Lily tugged on her sleeve. 'Mummy, come on,' she said impatiently, bringing Inés back down to earth with a jolt. Was she really standing in the playground of her daughter's school, contemplating flirting with the headmaster? It was so … *inappropriate.* But being inappropriate once in a while felt good.

'I'd better go,' she said briskly, wrenching her eyes away from Raff's gaze. 'We'll see you soon.'

'Have a great time,' Raff said, and she was sure she could hear disappointment in his voice. She hurried off, bemused.

'Is he going to be your boyfriend, mummy?' Lily asked as Inés belted her into the car seat.

'Who? Mr Taylor? Don't be silly.' Lily was far too perceptive for her own good. She looked disappointed by her mother's answer and Inés briskly started to chat away about Spain and the airport, while Lily listened intently, soon forgetting Mr Taylor.

• • •

Erin and Caoimhe were already home, wolfing down Jane's sandwiches, their bags stacked up in the corner of the kitchen. The horses and equipment had been sent on ahead that morning, so the only thing left to do was to get to the airport. Kent's flowers took pride of place in the middle of the kitchen table. Caoimhe appeared not to have noticed and Jane would be too polite to ask, but Erin raised her eyebrows at her mother over the expanse of petals.

'Nice flowers, mum.'

'Yes, they are, aren't they?' Inés replied, giving away nothing. 'Eat up, I don't want to be late and have a mad rush at the airport. It isn't a long flight; we'll be there in time for bed.'

Erin didn't reply and went back to her sandwiches, though the expression in her eyes was distant. Inés knew Erin would already be worrying about the upcoming qualifiers, no doubt judging her abilities and finding them wanting.

While the girls were eating, Inés went out to the yard for one last look at the remaining horse, and breathed in the sweet country air. She trusted her grooms, but as Sod's Law dictated something would go wrong while they were away, Inés felt compelled to make countless last-minute checks and goodbyes. The pony she'd bought from Maria was still a little highly strung but settling, though it would take longer than a few weeks for it to get used to their routine, and to Erin. Whatever problems Chelsea had been having, Inés suspected they were more to do with rider than pony.

Inés took her time saying goodbye to Prince Philip, or Phil as the whole family affectionately called him. Phil was a small Welsh grey, a sassy gelding with plenty of spunk to counter his nineteen years. In spite of his age, he still won gymkhanas for the younger girls and loved competing. His wise face revealed pride in his role. He was a pro, he knew what was expected of him and he delivered with cheek; brazen but never insolent. He was a show- off, and partial to escape attempts – just to remind the Cullens not to take him for granted. George had nicknamed him 'Houdini', Inés remembered with a nostalgic grin as she scratched the pony affectionately between his ears. He was as much a part of the family as Spanky; the girls loved him. Erin had started riding him at the age of three and one by one, he'd taught each of the girls to ride.

Of all the animals, she had the fondest memories of Phil. He was small enough to get into the house through the main entrance. She knew this because she'd once found him eating her beautiful ceiling-high potted kentia palm plant, while the girls gave him a sponge bath. The tree had been in her hallway since she and George bought the house and when George saw the mess he'd raised hell, claiming there was something wrong with Phil and he needed to be sold. The tree never recovered, but they kept Phil.

Phil was a confidant to the girls, as well as Inés. His mane offered a soft comforting blanket to wipe away tears, his ears kept their secrets, and his warm body invigorated cold little fingers on mid-winter rides. There was nothing more special than the relationship between a pony and its human.

'No trying to get out while we're gone,' Inés warned him. Phil slowly cocked his head to one side.

Ambling back to the house, her nostalgia was interrupted by her phone. William again. She put the phone to her ear with foreboding. Inés wasn't expecting this to be anything good. She was still angry at how he was so open to accusation and manipulation from that arsehole. And after knowing Inés for all those years and Mark for just a few. Though she wouldn't admit it, her ego was sorely bruised from his words.

'Hello,' she said briskly.

'Inés, it's William. Apologies for bothering you again.'

I hope it's not more unfounded accusations, she wanted to say. Instead, she went with: 'I hope it's nothing serious?' keeping her voice smooth, although she could feel anxiety fizzing in her tummy.

'I suppose it is. I phoned you to apologise.'

'Oh?' Inés was shocked. William had never been known to apologise to anyone, for anything, even after he'd reduced employees to tears with his dressing-downs.

'Yes. I've been thinking about what you said the other night, and you're right, I jumped the gun by questioning you like that. Your business is your business, and I trust you'd be honest with us if there was any problem that would compromise your reputation. If you need any help navigating the tax office, do let me know.'

'Thank you,' Inés said quietly. 'I appreciate that. And if I need any help, I'll ask.' *See*, she thought, *occasionally you catch more flies with honey than vinegar.*

'I've decided to heed your advice and send Mark to America. After talking with him further, it's clear he resents not moving up as quickly as he'd like – I suspect that was behind his underhand attempt to get you into trouble.'

I did try to tell you. But there was no point in being antagonistic when the situation was now clearly going her way. 'Does he know this?'

'Yes, I just got off the phone with him. He says he's pleased. He thinks he can *have more impact* overseas.'

Or he knows that his efforts to catch me with my pants down have failed.

'That may be for the best,' Inés agreed. This stunt had placed Mark on Inés' radar as someone who needed to be 'handled'. She doubted that his acts of sabotage would have stopped there. And after she'd sat and lunched with him, given him relationship advice, and listened to his problems on more than one occasion. She had no doubt he'd stop at nothing.

Inés shook her head. All this time he was waiting for her to trip up.

Never forget, Inés. The simpering ones are the silent assassins. With that thought in mind, she decided to text Mark and make sure he left the country under the impression everything was fine between them.

'Yes, well, enjoy your trip to Spain. I anticipate Mark will be in America by the time you return. We'll need someone to fill the role temporarily, so I trust you can assist in the recruitment process.'

'Of course. Thank you.'

Inés returned to the house feeling as though a weight had been lifted.

Erin was still in the kitchen with Caoimhe, looking less gloomy and more suspicious, eyeing her mother as she walked in.

'What's wrong, sweetheart?'

'Granny said those flowers were from Uncle Kent,' she said, looking distinctly unimpressed.

Once again, Inés inwardly cursed her mother. 'That's right. I bumped into him the other night at the de Bohuns'. He said to say hello to you all.'

'I like Uncle Kent,' Caoimhe announced. 'You should marry him next, mum, he's pretty rich.'

'Is that all you think about, Caoimhe?' Inés said.

Erin looked horrified and cut in. 'He's dad's friend! Is that why he's sending you flowers, mum?'

'No one's marrying anyone,' Inés said in a soothing voice. 'We may go out for dinner at some point, but that's hardly a wedding, is it?'

Erin pouted and looked away, staring out of the window.

'Come on girls,' Inés said chirpily, trying to lighten Erin's mood. 'Let's go to Spain!'

Chapter Eleven

Inés looked out of the window, watching the clouds below her, a fluffy blanket thrown across the sky turning rosy with sunset. Through a little break she could see the vast blue of the ocean and the sight soothed her. Even though she was a frequent flyer with both work and the girls' competing, being suspended in the sky never failed to invigorate her, no matter how much she travelled.

The coming days were just what Inés' nerves needed. The welling of pressure from work, competitions, financial problems and emotions in England grew more distant with each passing mile. They had two days for the horses to rest and acclimatise before the show started, and Inés was hoping for at least some time to relax around the pool.

It had certainly been earned. She'd been single-handedly responsible for creating an investment strategy in medium-sized property developments – foreseeing the fall and subsequent rise of the market – for their current shareholders, which in turn attracted big investors from China and the US. The key was hitting this at the right time. It took careful planning, and a gut reaction. She thoroughly expected another change in position soon; she couldn't move any higher up without becoming a partner.

The result would be a posting in America, which came with its own emotional barriers, but it was only a matter of time before they sent her out there to teach and learn. She'd hold them off for as long as she could, but her time was running out. She'd always excelled at work, thanks to her knack for smart, quick decisions and a natural head for business and finance. Her obsession with the smallest of details paid off and meant she received a lot of interest from other corporations looking for new blood.

It's a shame, she thought as she stretched her legs out as far as the business-class recliner would go, *that I can't apply those same skills to my love life.*

On paper, Kent was the more solid investment. He was wealthy, successful, and she'd known him for years. Raff was totally unsuitable, which might be why he intrigued her so much. She'd met a lot of men like Kent, but head teachers with soulful eyes and secret noble lineages? Not so many – Raff was a wild card. Inés hadn't got to where she had in life by taking uncalculated risks. *But then,* she mused, *perhaps it's time to let my hair down.* There was certainly chemistry between her and Raff, but wasn't that exactly how she was feeling about Kent too? *It's too confusing.*

She glanced at Lily sleeping in the seat next to her, her head on Jane's shoulder. Jane was reading *Good Housekeeping*, her hands gripping the pages tightly. Inés knew her nanny didn't like flying, but pride stopped her from admitting it.

Behind them, Erin and Caoimhe had their heads buried

in books; although Erin looked as though she was about to fall asleep too. Satisfied everyone was well, Inés pulled her silk eye mask over her face and decided to take a nap.

She was dozing when a voice came from a few rows behind. 'You expect me to eat this? I don't think it's much to ask for a decent meal after the amount of money I've paid for this flight.'

Inés groaned, recognising the voice and its owner immediately. Maria. *Of course she'd be on this plane.* It was only because they'd arrived late at the airport that they hadn't spotted her. Hoping Maria hadn't also chosen the same hotel she had, Inés dozed off.

• • •

They arrived at their carefully chosen, luxurious five-star hotel later that night only to walk straight into Maria in the hotel foyer. She gave a shriek of faux delight when she spotted Inés, and rushed over. Inés smiled politely.

'Maria. Good to see you again,' she said, offering her cheek for Maria's barely-there air kiss.

'You too, darling. Oh, isn't it such good fun that we're in the same hotel?' Maria's voice dripped with insincerity and Inés smiled tightly. She was tired and wanted to get up to their suite and lie down in the queen-sized bed that awaited her.

'Quite. No doubt I'll see you at breakfast?'

'Oh, we'll have ours in our room. I like to lie in when I can. It's important to stay rested, you know. Especially at your age, Inés.'

Knowing damn well that Maria wasn't much younger than her, Inés swallowed down a retort and instead ignored Maria's obvious jibe. She'd learned it was usually the best way with her; Maria relied on being able to get a rise out of people and it bothered her that Inés acted oblivious to her cattiness.

'Come on, mum,' Erin said, shooting Maria an annoyed look. Inés gave Maria a smile and turned away, motioning for a concierge to help them upstairs with their bags.

The suite she'd booked was as beautiful as Inés' secretary had suggested. Erin and Caoimhe cooed over the huge hot tub and the balcony that overlooked the swimming pool before running into the bedroom they'd be sharing. Jane was happy with her single room, and said goodnight almost before she'd put her suitcase in there.

'The flight has worn you out,' Inés observed sympathetically.

Jane nodded with a grimace. 'I wish I could get used to flying, but it doesn't agree with me,' she said, shaking her head. Inés didn't think it was the time to mention her upcoming flight to Sweden with Caoimhe.

Lily tugged at her hand and yawned loudly, and Inés picked her up, stroking her hair. 'I'll take Lily in with me tonight,' she told Jane, who looked grateful before closing her bedroom door behind her.

After she'd settled Lily, and while Erin and Caoimhe were trying out the hot tub, Inés poured herself a small glass of wine and sat out on the balcony. The moon was coming up over the mountains, glinting off the surface of the pool below, and the stars were bright in the clear Spanish sky. *Beautiful*, Inés thought as she took another sip. As much as it could be fiendishly hard work juggling her career and the children, at moments like this she could admit the hard work had certainly paid off. Inés had always been so afraid of being unable to afford things or being poor that she'd vowed as a child she never would be, and neither would she rely on anyone else to provide for her and her family.

Inés remembered her grandma, and how she'd suffered multiple mental breakdowns that had eventually led to her suicide when Inés was twelve. Her grandfather had been a cruel man, and although Inés was too young to understand their relationship, she knew that she, her mother and her grandmother were afraid of him. Inés thought things would have been different for her grandma had she been able to leave him, but there was no option for her to do that.

They spent most of the next day lazing around the pool. Thankfully, Maria was nowhere to be seen. Inés was catching up on work emails through oversized Prada sunglasses when Elizabeth messaged her with an invitation to a nearby flamenco bar that night with the other equestrian parents. Inés showed the message to Erin, who lay prone on the sunlounger next to her. Lily, Caoimhe and Jane were splashing each other in the shallow end of the pool.

'Want to come?' Inés asked. Erin was getting older, after all, and it would give Inés an excuse to leave early without seeming rude. 'You can have a glass of wine – a small one.'

Erin raised her eyebrows. 'I don't think so.'

'Fine. So you're going to let me deal with Elizabeth and Maria by myself?'

Erin chuckled. 'You'll be fine, mum. If anything, they're intimidated by you. That's why Maria is such a bitch. What will you wear?'

Inés ran through the outfits that she'd packed in her mind, pleased that Erin was taking an interest as fashion usually went straight over her head. Caoimhe was the same; they lived in jodhpurs and jogging pants and they were both gangly and unruly in their physique. Inés was reassured by their immaturity; there was plenty of time for them to grow up and there was no going back after that happened.

'I have a new silk jumpsuit,' she remembered. It still had the tags on.

Erin nodded authoritatively. 'Wear that. Maria will hate it.'

Inés went to admonish Erin but instead paused and agreed. Her daughter was now nearly a woman and fast moving from child into best friend. 'Good idea,' she agreed.

That evening as she admired herself in the mirror, she had to admit Erin was right; Maria would hate it. The jumpsuit fitted Inés like a dream. It highlighted her olive skin and brought out the green flecks in her eyes. Wearing her new Christian Louboutin shoes and tasteful diamond earrings, she threw a short black leather jacket over her shoulders and grabbed her matching Yves Saint Laurent clutch. She looked amazing. Certainly good enough to hold her own amongst the other yummy mummies.

As they were in the same hotel, it made sense for Maria and Inés to walk to the flamenco bar together, so she waited downstairs in the foyer, noticing the admiring looks from the hotel staff. The elevator doors opened and Maria appeared, in a white shift dress and what looked like pink diamonds at her neck. Inés offered a smile and tried to inject genuine warmth into it; she was intending to have a good night and didn't want to spend it trying to navigate whatever rivalry Maria thought they had.

Maria, however, had other ideas. She looked Inés up and down with feigned surprise. 'You're wearing red? That's brave.'

'It's a Bishaaro,' Inés told her, gratified when Maria's cheeks flushed.

'I know she's supposed to be the next big thing,' Maria said quickly. 'But I don't rate her; I think her designs are a little gaudy.' She looked pointedly at Inés' outfit.

Inés felt sympathy for Maria. The rumour in their social circle was that Maria's upbringing had been both entitled and miserable. As a child, she'd been a pawn in her parents' marriage and surrounded by sycophants. No wonder she acted as she did. She was doomed to repeat her parents' failures. 'Well, you look lovely. Let's have a good night, shall we? Before the stress of the competition starts,' Inés said firmly.

Maria blinked, looking suitably chastened, and followed Inés out of the hotel without another word. She remained quiet on the way to the flamenco bar, as though searching for something to say that wasn't injected with aggression. Nice words failing her, they remained in silence the entire walk.

They found the bar and were greeted loudly by Elizabeth de Bohun and three other mums who were part of their messenger group. One of them, Molly, looked pleased to see Inés, and they embraced warmly. Molly was around the same age as Inés, and far more outspoken and direct with people like Maria. She came from a farm in Herefordshire where she and her husband had made their living buying and selling horses. Inés had done business with her before and had found her trustworthy and a straight-dealer, though still a shrewd business woman. If she'd taken a different path, she'd have been much more successful.

'Did I tell you that Inés is my neighbour?' Elizabeth asked, air kissing Inés loudly. She already smelled of alcohol, so much so that Inés wondered how early in the day she'd started drinking. *Did Guy not notice – or care?*

They found a booth and were soon served by a dark and handsome waiter who looked slightly older than their children. He was clearly taken with Maria, as he hovered around her trying to win her attention with flashes of a confident smile. Maria ignored him and he eventually left her alone. He couldn't have been more than twenty.

'I wonder who else will make the team this year,' Elizabeth said, suppressing a hiccup. 'Of course, dear Ben must be chosen, he's worked so hard.'

'You must be worried about Erin, Inés?' Maria said silkily.

'Worried? Why would I be?'

'Well, she's had a patchy year, hasn't she? Not up to her usual standards.'

There was a hush around the table and Inés felt a warm rush of rage. No one won every show – in fact Maria's daughter had only just managed to scrape through all year. It was also an unspoken rule that, on a night out like this, they didn't discuss their children, who at this stage were rivals for places on the team.

'Erin is absolutely fine,' Inés said in a voice that brooked no arguments; the same voice she used at work when closing a tough deal. Maria looked down at her glass, without having the grace to seem even a little abashed.

'She's such a bitch,' Molly said to Inés, not caring who heard.

Elizabeth broke the awkward silence with a delighted yelp as she spotted a man at the bar. 'Jack! Darling! Do come and join us. Shove up, girls, and let him sit down. We could do with some testosterone over here.'

'And that is some testosterone,' Maria murmured, sitting very straight and flicking back her long blonde hair. Her cheekbones looked even sharper than Inés remembered, and she wondered if she'd had some work done; she did look good. Inés was contemplating getting more done herself. She'd had a boob job in between the twins and Lily.

But the man who crossed over the room towards them

had his eyes fixed on Inés. For a moment she wondered where she'd previously met him, then realised he was the official from Erin's qualifying show.

'Would you ladies like a drink?' he asked politely, although he was looking directly at Inés. It was a bold stare, full of promise, yet not sleazy. Inés felt a flutter of excitement. It wasn't the done thing to flirt with an official on the team … but it was hardly unheard of, either. Inés felt flattered that his interest was clearly directed at her.

'We've only just ordered, but join us,' Elizabeth enthused. She moved a little more to let him into the booth. 'Come on girls, shove up I say!'

In the scramble, Maria scooted over to Jack so she was practically sitting in his lap. Molly caught Inés' gaze and rolled her eyes, and Inés suppressed a smile. The others were now hanging off Jack's every word, which Inés found amusing, considering she was the only single one.

'Shall we dance?' Inés asked Molly as the band kicked up some salsa. As she wriggled out of the booth, she felt Jack's eyes on her. She continued to feel them as she swayed to the music, burning through her clothes and warming her skin as much as the cocktail had.

'He's watching you,' Molly said, flicking her hip.

'I know,' Inés said with a grin, rolling her body seductively. A few songs later they resumed their seats, and Jack smiled at her. 'You move well,' he said. 'Natural rhythm. Do you dance?'

'Only for fun,' Inés said. It was Maria's eyes that she could feel on her now, but they were decidedly more hostile than Jack's languid gaze. Feeling bold, and spurred on by Maria's rivalry, Inés took her last sip and slid her empty glass towards Jack. 'I'll have that drink now, thank you,' she said. His eyes twinkled at her.

'And me,' Maria said quickly, knocking back her glass. 'I'll come to the bar with you, Jack.' She stood up quickly and all but clambered over Elizabeth, who was sinking lower into her seat, clearly the worse for wear.

'Elizabeth,' Molly said tactfully, 'you look awfully tired. Me too; I get terrible jet lag. Shall we walk back to our hotel?'

Elizabeth blinked at Molly as though struggling to process what the other woman was saying. 'Back?' she slurred. 'The night is still young.' She squinted at Molly as though struggling to focus, then reached into her handbag. She missed the opening twice and looked down at her bag, confused. Then she hiccupped. 'Maybe I *should* get back,' she said, getting to her feet. She was swaying.

'Great idea!' Molly enthused. 'Come on; I'll walk back with you.' She winked at Inés as she discreetly led Elizabeth out of the bar by her arm. The other two mums decided to leave with them, leaving Inés sitting alone as she waited for Maria and Jack to return. They soon came over, Maria with her arm looped through Jack's. She slid in the booth after him, so close that she was once again nearly in his lap. Inés pretended not to notice and accepted her drink gracefully.

'Thank you. You're very kind.'

'My pleasure,' said Jack, gazing into her eyes as he

smiled at her, revealing a dimple near the corner of his mouth. Inés decided that a brief fling in Spain might be what she needed to get out of the dating limbo she'd been in for so long. Then, perhaps, she could make a clearer decision about Kent.

'So, you're single, Inés?' Jack asked.

Inés nodded demurely. 'Yes. My husband passed away four years ago.'

'I'm sorry,' he said politely, then added: 'That's a long time to be alone. Especially for such a beautiful woman.'

Inés lifted one shoulder in a graceful shrug. 'I've been so busy with the children, work and the yard, I don't get the time,' she confessed. 'They're all at school now, and though I'm incredibly busy, I miss having them around the house.'

'I imagine a single mother of five children would be enough to put any man off,' Maria piped up, an unmistakable catty edge to her voice. 'Don't you think so, Jack?'

With his eyes still on Inés, Jack shook his head. 'Not at all. I think it would take more than that to put a man off a woman like Inés.'

Inés tried not to smile at the look of outrage on Maria's face.

'I'll leave you two lovebirds to it,' Maria huffed. 'The night is turning out to be rather dull.'

'Should we walk you back?' Inés offered, but Maria shook her head.

'I'll be all right,' she snapped, 'it's only down the road. I wouldn't want to be playing third wheel now, would I?'

Jack stood up to let her out, frowning as he watched her go. He sat back down, opposite Inés, and gave a confused smile. 'She seems a little, er, put out?'

'Mmmm,' Inés answered, taking a sip of her drink. Not wanting to come across as bitchy, she refrained from saying that Maria couldn't bear someone else being the centre of attention. Especially if the bestower of that attention was a man as handsome as Jack.

'So, it looks as though it's just me and you,' he said, an undertone to his voice that made Inés tingle. 'Would you like to dance?'

'Why not?' Inés stood up and made her way to the dance floor, aware of Jack close behind her. The band were playing a slow, bachata beat and Inés let her body move to the music, losing herself in it. Jack moved in time with her, completely unselfconscious. He took her hand into his, her slender fingers clasping the nook between his thumb and forefinger, while his other slid down her painfully slowly, coming to rest eventually on the small of her back. They danced close together, creating their own steps to the exotic music that pulsed between them.

'You're a pretty good mover,' Inés noted. Jack raised an eyebrow, lending the comment an obvious innuendo. Inés held his gaze as she swayed, feeling the heat rising between their close bodies, enjoying it. *What harm could it do if she threw caution to the wind for one night?* The girls were safe with Jane, she was in a beautiful foreign country, and she'd hardly be the first parent to have a bit of fun with an official. In that regard, Inés had been completely tame over the years. The cocktails were no doubt affecting her judgement.

They danced for a while, the songs becoming slightly faster into pounding beats. Inés raised her hands over her head and moved her hips, much to Jack's obvious delight. They returned to their booth and Inés finished her drink.

Inés knew where this night was going. This is what she wanted to do, this was going to happen, and she'd enjoy every moment of it. Now committed, nothing was going to stop her.

'I'll go to the bar this time,' she said, starting to stand up though feeling as if she needed to sit down for longer. Jack reached over the table and laid a hand over hers. She glanced down at his tanned fingers, feeling excited with every touch he offered her.

'How about we get a drink at my hotel?' he asked.

Inés paused before answering. 'Sounds fun,' she said softly.

Jack tried and failed to restrain his grin of delight. His eyes sparkled with desire. Then he stood up and, thankfully, offered Inés his arm. They made their way through the bar to the street outside. It was lit up with moonlight and the lamps outside the bars and the scent of the sea rolled in from the beach and a soft breeze caressed Inés' bare shoulders. The midnight air was still warm. Inés savoured the sensations, feeling a sense of freedom. She held on to Jack's arm, stealing glimpses of his face as they walked. His free hand lightly traced the most teasing of movements on her forearm as they enjoyed their walk. Inés could feel herself responding – her skin was goose-pimpling, her breathing shorter and erratic. She was excited and couldn't wait to see what the rest of Jack's body looked like. Inés suddenly became hungry for him and wanted his body close to hers.

Jack was staying at the hotel not far from hers, in a luxury single room that had a hot tub and balcony to rival her own. While he fixed them a drink from the minibar, Inés walked out on to the balcony. It overlooked a pretzel-shaped swimming pool that was lit up with classic white lights and she had the urge to dive into it, using the cool water to alleviate the agitation building through her senses. Invigorated by a gust of wind that tousled her hair, she leaned back to look at the stars in the clear sky and smiled.

Jack appeared next to her, holding out her drink. She winced as the bitter liquid burned her throat and tried not to cough. 'Goodness, that's strong. Are you trying to get me drunk?' She laughed lightly.

Jack smiled, his voice low and full of promise when he spoke. 'Do I need to?'

She looked him straight in the eyes, the heat rising between them. 'No, Jack,' she replied in a whisper. 'You don't.'

He stepped towards her and leaned in, gently brushing her lips with his. Inés felt a jolt of electricity go through her entire body and her nerve endings lit up as though his kiss had triggered something from deep within. The excitement of having another man's lips on hers, wanting her. Her desire ignited further with his kiss deepening. It had been far too long since she'd allowed herself to feel like this.

Jack stepped back, watching her closely. Stroking her cheek, he allowed his fingers to trail down her neck. Inés shivered as he lightly cupped her breast. She leaned towards him and he smiled.

'Let's go inside; you're getting cold,' he said.

Inés nodded. The bubble of nerves and excitement made a cocktail in her stomach and Iné s felt as though she was walking on air. She stumbled as she stepped through the glass door and Jack briefly caught her arm, steadying her. Inés sat on the small chaise longue opposite the bed, setting her shoes neatly on the carpet before tucking her legs up beneath. She patted the seat.

It feels nice.

Jack immediately sat next to her and rested his hand on her thigh as though it were perfectly natural that it should be there.

It feels nice.

'You're stunning,' Jack told her, slipping an arm around her shoulders. 'You were the envy of every woman in that club tonight … and me of every man.'

Corny, but who cares?

Inés tipped her head towards his as he leaned in to kiss her again. No need to analyse it. She wanted this to happen.

Jack gave a low groan before kissing Inés hungrily, and she locked her arms around his neck. He slid his hand down her body to cup her buttocks and pull her body closer into his. Then his hand was running through her hair while Inés tipped her head back, and Jack moved his lips down, kissing her neck, delicately grazing her skin with his teeth.

Inés moaned from low down in her throat as she felt excitement build from deep inside her. It seemed to urge Jack on and he moved faster, sliding a thigh between Inés' own. And now they were kissing with a raw and urgent passion that took Inés' breath away. Jack fumbled to undo her jumpsuit and she pushed him aside for a brief moment so she could wriggle out of the top and free her breasts. Jack pulled back to look at her, his eyes dark with desire.

Then he jumped to his feet and held out his hand. Inés stood up and stepped out of her jumpsuit, standing in front of him wearing nothing but a scrap of red lace that only just passed for underwear. She took his hand and waited. Jack smiled and raised his eyebrows.

Inés reached for his shirt and began to slowly undo the buttons. She leaned forward and dropped a slow trail of kisses down his exposed chest. But Jack couldn't wait and he grabbed at his shirt and pulled it off, flinging it aside.

He had a natural tan, broad shoulders, impressive biceps and a deliciously taut, rippled abdominal wall with a sparse smattering of dark hair that disappeared tantalisingly below his waistband. *Too tantalisingly.* Inés tugged at his belt, unbuckling it and sliding it out of the loops, dropping it on the ground behind her. Jack stepped out of his trousers to reveal tight white cotton shorts, thick, hard thighs and an impressive bulge.

Inés' heart was beating so hard and fast, she was sure he could hear it.

Jack picked Inés up carefully and carried her over to the huge bed. He lay her down on the soft blankets and knelt between her thighs, looking up at her with a question in his eyes. Inés nodded. *Yes, that's what I want. Now.*

She lifted her hips so he could slide her panties down her thighs and off her legs. Then she sighed in anticipation of what was to come.

Okay, not quite like that … but maybe he needed a moment to get it right.

Inés wriggled so Jack knew exactly where he should focus. It made no difference. She put one hand down and gently pushed his head to the left. That's where he needed to be. He moved back the moment she lifted her hand.

Inés stared at the ceiling. A final determined wriggle did nothing. He was poking at her as if she was a slab of meat. Licking and patting as if he was following a manual that only he had read. And now he was speeding up as if he had to get moving or he'd miss his train.

She didn't give up that easily. Inés shifted her hips pointedly to give him a better angle. Made an 'oooh' sound and faked a gasp of pleasure when he almost got it right.

It made no difference. Jack was going to do what Jack was going to do and she might as well have not been there. Inés stifled a yelp of pain when in his eagerness he pinched a bit of skin.

The final drops of desire trickled out of Inés and she now felt frustrated. *This was hurting.*

Inés wriggled away and pulled Jack towards her, guiding his hand to where his mouth had been. Unfortunately, he was no more dexterous with his fingers than he had been with his tongue, so Inés quickly gave up that idea, and pushed him on to his back. Jack grabbed at a condom from his nightstand and hastened to put it on, the latex making slapping noises as he hurried.

Jack's eyes lit up as he grabbed her hips and rocked against her. 'You liked that, didn't you?' he said triumphantly.

Which planet is he on?

'Mmm,' Inés muttered, wondering how quickly she could get this over with. At least now she was in charge and could control the pace. Inés screwed her eyes closed. She ignored Jack's idiotic declarations of sexual prowess and attempts to speed her up. She moved as she needed to, feeling the tension grow, her insides coiling in anticipation of release.

Then Jack let out a sudden bellow, his fingers stabbed into her hip bones and he thrust up into her, his whole body shuddering. He stopped and smiled up at her lazily, looking like a cat who'd got the cream.

'That was amazing, wasn't it?' he said.

'Not really,' Inés answered nonchalantly.

Jack ignored the comment and shimmied out from beneath her, heading straight to the bathroom.

Was that it?

Jack was singing to himself in the bathroom as she lay on her back, staring at the ceiling and wishing she'd brought her vibrator. Or, better yet, that she'd gone straight back to her hotel when Molly and Elizabeth had left.

Sleeping would have been a much better use of her time.

Chapter Twelve

Inés woke up with the sun streaming through the window and a pounding head. She removed her eye mask and sat up gingerly, wincing at the bright light. Next to her, Lily mumbled and rolled over, her plump body snuggling into her mother's. For a moment, Inés felt disoriented, and then the events of last night came rushing back.

Jack had wanted to have sex again, after twenty minutes of talking about himself, but Inés, seeing no reason to expect the second time would be any better than the first, had excused herself and left. She'd walked the short distance back to her hotel alone, let herself in and fell asleep in her bed almost immediately. At some point, Lily had climbed into bed with her.

Jack hadn't wanted her to go, insisting she stay until morning so he could take her for breakfast, and he'd looked sulky when Inés had insisted. There was no way she was going to let the girls wake up to her not being there, not without advance warning. He hadn't understood. In fact, he'd rolled over in the bed and not even offered to walk her out. Inés had pulled on her by now terribly crumpled outfit and made her way back, trying not to let his petulance ruin what had otherwise been a good night. She couldn't wait to tell Chris and Tabby. In fact, she thought they would be proud of her for finally taking their advice – though they would commiserate with her on what a let-down it had been.

Regardless of her disappointment and guilt, she couldn't help but feel proud of herself on her walk home.

In the cold light of morning, however, she was reaping the consequences of her impulsive decision. Her head was going like a jackhammer. She got out of bed and rummaged through her suitcase, certain she'd put some painkillers other than Lily's Calpol in there. Grabbing at a pack of ibuprofen, she took two out and then went over to the kitchenette to fix herself a glass of water.

Her handbag was by the sink where she must have left it last night – or to be more accurate, earlier that morning – and as she swallowed her tablets she heard her phone vibrating inside it. She pulled it out, frowning when she saw it was Jack, and it was only 7 am. *Hadn't he slept?* She ignored it, deciding to speak to him later after breakfast and when her head had cleared. But as the screen cleared, she saw that she had a string of missed calls from him.

Ten, to be exact.

Assuming something was wrong she dialled back, wondering what on earth could have happened for him to call ten times in the last thirty minutes.

'Hello,' she said as he picked up. 'Is everything okay?'

'Let me take you for breakfast. I'll pick you up in twenty minutes.'

Inés wasn't sure whether to be flattered at the fact he was clearly smitten with her, or creeped out by his eagerness. 'I can't, Jack. The girls will be up soon.'

'You have a nanny, don't you?' he said, in a slightly condescending tone that put Inés' teeth on edge. She resented his assumption that having a nanny meant she'd leave her girls at any available opportunity.

'I can't do breakfast, Jack. I'm sorry,' Inés said firmly.

'Lunch, then,' Jack said. 'We won't get much of a chance to spend time together when the shows start.'

Inés didn't know what to say. She hadn't thought beyond last night, and had certainly had no expectations other than one or two passion-filled nights. Breakfasts and lunch dates had been the last thing on her mind. Now, in the cold light of morning, after such a disappointing encounter, she had no desire whatsoever to repeat it again. She was shocked that Jack was turning out to be the clingy type, too. 'Mummy?' Behind her, Lily sat up in bed.

'I have to go,' Inés said hurriedly. 'I'll call you later, okay?' She put the phone down on Jack's protestations and climbed back into bed to cuddle Lily. On the counter, her phone started to vibrate again. Inés ignored it.

'Your phone, mummy,' Lily yawned, winding her chubby arms around her mother's neck, still cosy in her half-dream world.

'It doesn't matter,' Inés assured her. The phone stopped vibrating, then started again a few seconds later. It couldn't be Jack, surely? Not when she'd already told him she was busy. Worrying it might be Alice or one of the twins, she got back out of bed and picked up the phone. Two missed calls from Jack.

Inés switched it off and went back to bed, her headache increasing in spite of the ibuprofen. She didn't need this when she had to concentrate on helping Erin make the team. Perhaps it had been a mistake to go back to his hotel. Jack had seemed both handsome and sophisticated at the time, but this was starting to blow up in her face. Besides, it was done and she didn't need to beat herself up about bad choices that were so irrelevant. A lunch date might actually have been nice, but the twelve phone calls and obvious sense of entitlement was hardly endearing.

After everyone was up and had gone down for a delicious continental breakfast, Inés and Erin went to view the ring where she'd be competing the next day. Erin seemed even more tense than usual, her face white as she surveyed the jumps. The course looked as difficult as would be expected at this level, but Inés was confident that Erin would do well. Or she would, if she could access some of that confidence for herself.

'It's a difficult course, mum,' Erin said under her breath, her jaw set in that way which showed she was clamping her teeth together with stress.

The cycle of defeat before even stepping into the ring felt endless as they surveyed the course of jumps, but it was Inés' job to rub out that emotion for her daughter.

'Any particular parts worrying you?' Inés asked briskly,

knowing that simply trying to reassure Erin when she was in this mindset would make the situation grow into something it needn't be. Erin nodded, motioning towards a huge water jump.

'Baby isn't great with those. I know we've focused on them this year, but that jump is a monster, and that's a bloody big upright afterwards.'

Inés levelled. 'I see what you mean. This'll be difficult but it's certainly achievable. He was so good at the water jump at the qualifier, wasn't he? So, we know the capability is there. You just need to attack and hold him together in between.' Coddling her with 'you'll be fines' and 'believe in yourselfs' wouldn't cut it. She continued: 'I'm sure the other competitors will be thinking the same thing when they see it. Ben de Bohun has been losing form the past few weeks; I wonder how he'll handle it?'

'Speak of the devil,' Erin murmured. Inés turned to see Elizabeth and Maria walking towards them, arm in arm as though suddenly best of friends, with Ben and Maria's daughter, Chelsea, trailing behind, looking bored. With that attitude, their place on the team would be under pressure.

As they got closer, Inés could see the bags under Elizabeth's eyes and wondered how painful her hangover was that morning. Elizabeth smiled at her weakly and with a touch of embarrassment, Inés thought. Maria, on the other hand, simply glared at her.

'Have a nice time with Jack last night?' she sniped. Her forehead, filled with Botox, was shining in the sun.

'Yes, thank you,' said Inés lightly, offering an innocent smile. She had nothing to be ashamed of.

Maria sniffed loudly and turned towards the ring, while Elizabeth gave Inés a glazed smile. 'I think the heat went to my head last night,' she said. 'Bless dear Molly for seeing me back to the hotel.'

'I didn't think it was that hot last night,' Erin said innocently. Inés elbowed her discreetly in the ribs as Elizabeth went bright red and pulled her sunglasses down from her head on to her eyes, then turned to survey the ring with Maria. Ben and Chelsea seemed to be more interested in looking at something on Ben's phone.

'Aren't you going to check the jumps out, Ben?' Inés asked. He looked up at her startled, as though the idea hadn't occurred to him.

'There's a nasty turn,' Erin offered, trying to be friendly.

Chelsea smirked, pushing her platinum hair back off her face. She was a younger version of Maria; beautiful, intimidating, and just as spoilt. 'You must be worried then; you were nearly disqualified before because of a turn, weren't you? I hope you've learned to pace yourself.'

Inés felt Erin stiffen next to her and opened her mouth to retort something in defence of her daughter, but Chelsea was already sauntering away to stand next to her mother. Ben followed, his eyes blatantly on Chelsea's bottom. *That explained why he had such little interest in the ring*, Inés thought. Adolescent hormones were clearly winning out over ambition.

'Can we go now, mum?' Erin said quietly, a note of pleading in her tone. She'd let Chelsea get to her.

'Yes, darling. Let's take the horses out for a short stroll, shall we? They need a warm-up and I'm sure the grooms would like an hour off.' She led Erin away, pausing to wave at Elizabeth who gave them a sickly smile of farewell.

'Do you think I should say something to Guy about her drinking?' Inés asked Erin as soon as they were out of earshot.

Erin shrugged. 'Rather you than me, mum.' Erin paused. 'I suspect he knows anyway. He must do. He has to live with her.'

'I don't think he's at home a lot.' *Perhaps Elizabeth was lonely?* Inés resolved that when they returned, she'd make the effort to visit her more. As infuriating as she often found the de Bohun family, they'd been good neighbours in her most desperate time, offering emotional support when George had died, which extended above and beyond neighbourly interest.

As they walked towards the stables, Inés felt her phone ringing and pulled it out of her beach bag. Jack. Again. She'd managed to rid herself of one headache, she didn't want to invite another in. But she thought it best to meet this head on and answer. Slowing a little to allow Erin the lead, she answered it, aiming to sound friendly but without being flirtatious, in the hope he'd take the hint.

'Jack! How's things?'

'Inés, I can't stop thinking about last night. You were absolutely amazing,' he said in a sensual tone that made

Inés want to vomit all over her beautifully comfortable Tod's. She wasn't attracted to him anymore. The fact that he'd been so oblivious to her lack of pleasure last night, coupled with the expectation she'd automatically want to see him again a matter of hours later – not to mention his complete dismissal of her children – had robbed him of any residual charm.

She tilted her head back to save her shoes and reached for something inane to say. 'Oh, thank you,' she said, 'but I'm with my daughter at the moment.' Erin, ever observant, hung back and was peering at her curiously.

'So, I'll pick you up for lunch in an hour,' he said, a statement rather than a question, which made Inés flush with annoyance.

'Like I said,' she replied, trying not to sound snappy, 'I'm busy. I'm afraid I won't be able to do lunch today.'

There was a loaded silence at the other end of the phone. 'I see,' Jack said eventually, and his tone was now cold. 'You're blowing me out.'

'It's nothing personal. I'm tied up. It's not quite a holiday, after all. I'm sure you've got lots to do, yourself?'

'Oh, don't worry,' Jack said in a voice so dripping with sarcasm that he suddenly reminded her of Maria. 'I'm sure I can entertain myself elsewhere.'

'Sounds like a great idea,' Inés said breezily. 'I must go. Bye then.' She placed her phone back in her bag, shaking her head at the cheek of the man. Erin raised an eyebrow.

'It was Jack,' Inés told her. 'He wanted to take me out for lunch.' She wasn't going to lie to her daughter.

Erin looped her arm through hers. 'You're in demand at the moment, mum,' she said. 'Kent, Mr Taylor, now Jack. I bet Maria is jealous as hell.'

'Well, Maria doesn't know any of them except Jack,' Inés pointed out, 'and besides. Raff – Mr Taylor – is Lily's teacher. I don't know him outside the school.'

'Mum,' Erin said impatiently, 'literally everyone knows he likes you. Even Lily picked up on it, and she lives on her own planet at the best of times. You don't notice because he's not your usual type.'

Inés laughed. 'And how would you know what my type is, young lady?'

'Well, he's the opposite of dad … or Kent. Which is why I think it would be a great idea.'

'Thank you for the dating advice,' Inés teased. Erin shrugged and didn't reply. She showed a remarkable lack of interest in boys for sixteen, and Inés often wondered if it was because she was so hyper-focused on achievement.

After they'd exercised the horses, they met Jane, Caoimhe and Lily for lunch. Caoimhe was full of excitement about Sweden, and her enthusiasm was in stark contrast to Erin's brooding. Inés squeezed Erin's hand under the lunch table and Erin pulled her hand away in annoyance at their mother's mollycoddling.

'Can I go to Sweden with Nanny Jane and Caoimhe, mummy?' Lily asked, bouncing in her seat. With her Heidi plaits and sunglasses she looked adorable and Inés felt her heart melt as she smiled at her. She was so lucky to have her girls and to have such a good relationship with them all. Even the teenage years, so far at least, had seen no major disruption. *If only the girls still had their father around*, Inés thought wistfully, *things would be perfect.*

'Don't you want to stay in Spain? It won't be sunny like this in Sweden, and you won't have the pool,' Inés pointed out.

'I know,' Lily said, her face taking on a serious expression, 'but I want to see the Royal Palace and the Nobel Prize Museum. It will be good for my egg-cation, mummy. I learned about it in school. I'd like to practise my Swedish, too.'

'But you don't know any Swedish,' Inés smiled.

'That's why I need to practise,' Lily admonished seriously.

Caoimhe burst into laughter and playfully tugged at Lily's plaits. 'It's education, silly. Can she, mum?'

Inés hesitated, not sure how she felt about being separated from her youngest, even though it would only be for a few days. Still, Lily was a funny thing, often older than her years; an old soul in a young body. And if she had a fledgling interest in history, Inés wanted to nurture it. Though she probably was more tempted by the opportunities for adventure while with Jane and her sister, rather than the boring time Inés might offer.

'I suppose so,' Inés said, mock sternly, 'but you must be well behaved and do everything Nanny Jane says.'

'Thank you, mummy. This is great news for me!' Lily's sweet angelic voice tinkled in the air and she threw sticky arms around Inés' neck. After disentangling herself, Inés glanced at Erin, who looked lighter at the news. It would be good to have some time alone with her eldest daughter; Inés suspected Erin needed it, at least after the competitions were over and Erin could hopefully relax.

Inés tucked into a gorgeous Mediterranean salad, followed by an exquisitely made lime sorbet, and was sipping at her iced water when her phone once again buzzed angrily in her bag. Erin rolled her eyes as Inés pulled it out and grimaced. 'Is it that Jack again?'

'Yes,' said Inés with a sigh, deciding to turn her phone off for a while. She didn't like to, not with her mother and the twins still back in England, but the twins should be at school by now and hopefully Alice could manage to keep herself out of trouble. Besides, they had her work phone and hotel numbers. Hopefully, when Jack realised her phone was off, he'd get the message.

After lunch, they spent the afternoon around the pool. Molly came over to join them with her son Tristan, much to Inés' delight. Tristan always put a smile on Erin's face. He was also the one who could make her feel most at ease when discussing her riding form.

'Elizabeth looked the worse for wear this morning,' Inés said quietly as they watched the teenagers having fun on the water slides. Jane had taken Lily for a siesta and to pack their bags ready for Sweden.

Molly nodded as she took a long sip of her drink. 'I practically had to carry her up to her room,' she said with a sigh. 'She's definitely progressed from when I saw her last year. You live near her, don't you?'

'Yes. I'm going to go over and have a chat with her; see if I can offer my support. She can be an awful snob, but she's a good heart. I should have made a move sooner, but I guess I was too preoccupied.'

'Yes, I get that impression. I wouldn't say the same for that horrible son of hers. He always tries to make snide remarks to Tristan. He looks down on him because we, well, we're not quite the same as him, you know.'

'It's just his ego, because Tristan is a better rider than him. You know, to some of these kids every competition is an extension of themselves. And for someone like Ben, who needs to be on top – well, it's personal,' Inés said. She had no doubt that Tristan would be the first rider selected for the team, and Ben de Bohun's fragile self-esteem meant he didn't like anyone taking his limelight. 'I think he's met his match with Chelsea, though,' Inés mused, remembering how the boy had scampered after her at the ring that morning.

Molly laughed. 'We can hope. So, how did things go with Jack last night? You're being very coy.'

Making sure the kids were out of earshot, Inés told Molly about the ill-fated night and Jack's hounding of her on the phone. To demonstrate, she turned her phone on. Jack had left eight voice messages, asking her to go out with him again that evening, each more irate than the last. The final message sounded vaguely threatening. Molly shook her head in horror.

'I'd never have expected him to behave like this! You must have got under his skin, Inés.' Molly paused for a moment, then continued: 'I know you can't tell anyone within the teams about it, but you could tell the organisers of *this* show.'

'No point,' said Inés with a shrug. 'They'd think I was doing it out of spite. Or worse, that I'd slept with Jack to secure Erin's position.' She sighed. 'I've no idea why he's so interested. Last night was mediocre. And I'm being generous with the word "mediocre".' Inés stopped as the kids came over for a drink of water, wet from the pool and laughing. Erin looked the happiest she had since they had got here, and Inés hoped it lasted.

Molly stayed for another drink and then went back to her hotel with Tristan. Everyone would be getting an early night, ready for the big day tomorrow. This is where it stopped being a holiday and got serious. The online feeds would be full of motivational memes and pictures of their little darlings. The more wins, the more pictures. Inés tried to join in, enjoying the sense of community if nothing else, but she found the covert rivalry distasteful, and also didn't agree with splashing her kids all over social media. Erin, painfully awkward, would hate it.

She went back up to their hotel room with Erin to get changed and have a nap before ordering room service. Jane, Caoimhe and Lily would be leaving early the next morning, so everyone needed their sleep. Luckily, Jane had managed to get Lily on to their flight and upgrade their seats.

After a relaxing cool shower and a lie down on the bed with her book, a new thriller which was better than she'd been expecting, the girls jumped on the bed and they started looking through the menu. Erin and Caoimhe were soon arguing about what to order, and Inés stepped on to the balcony with her phone to call Alice and the twins. A brief conversation revealed the girls were busy with their homework and her mother was suffering terribly with her hips. Inés gingerly checked her texts and voice messages, relieved when there was nothing more from Jack. Perhaps he'd finally given up.

Her stomach sank when her phone promptly rang, but the number wasn't Jack's.

It was Kent.

'Hello,' Inés said, bemused but also pleased. His deep voice came rolling over the line, bringing with it a sense of familiarity.

'Inés. I'm in Spain.'

'Oh?' She couldn't get away from her admirers today.

'Yes, last minute business meeting. Very lucrative deal actually, and cause for a celebration I thought. So, I'm only a few miles down the road from you. I was wondering if you fancied lunch tomorrow before I fly home?'

'How far is a few miles?' she batted back flirtatiously, buying time to think.

'Well, about fifty, but I'd make the journey for you.'

Inés pondered. There was no denying she liked the idea – and in fact was more excited by it than she cared to analyse – but Erin and the trials were her first priority for the next few days.

She allowed a loaded silence to grow. 'Possibly. Erin is

competing first in the morning and again around noon. I could potentially do a late lunch, but it depends on how she does. I won't have a lot of time. Unless you're happy to come to me and we could meet in my hotel bar for half an hour?'

'Whatever works best for you. I know you're busy with the girls. It's one of the things I admire about you, Inés; you're a wonderful mother.'

'Thank you,' she responded, feeling flattered, as well as thinking how different his attitude was to Jack's, who apparently expected women – or perhaps anyone – to be at his beck and call.

'I'll drop you a message in the morning then,' Kent said, 'and best of luck for Erin in the morning. Give her my love, won't you?'

'I will,' Inés promised, keeping to herself that Erin would be less than receptive to it.

'Bye then, my darling,' Kent said in such an easily intimate tone that it left Inés at a loss for words. Only after she'd said goodbye and walked back into the bedroom did she realise she'd forgotten to thank him for the flowers.

Chapter Thirteen

Come on, Erin, you can do it. Inés leaned forward in her seat, holding her breath as Erin began her round. So far, her performance had lacked aggression, and she desperately needed to go clear in this round – and tomorrow – if she was going to show the team selectors what they could have for the British team. Erin was holding her own, but without pushing herself to the limit she wouldn't shine. So far among the Brits, Tristan was leading while Ben de Bohun and Erin were doing well, and Chelsea was catching up. Chelsea had certainly improved this year in overall points, but mainly through expensive, ready-made horses that she usually ruined after six months. But that didn't matter. All that mattered was numbers and experience.

Inés had never been one to begrudge anyone else's success, and she admired hard work, but it was hard not to feel disgruntled when Chelsea shot Erin sneering glances all morning, whispering and laughing with Ben whenever she went past. Inés was furious, but Erin wouldn't thank her for interfering. *This is a good lesson for Erin,* Inés thought, although it broke her heart to watch. *There'll always be people on the sidelines willing you to fail, and you will fail if you let them get into your head.*

All Inés wanted was for Erin to do her best. She was proud of her efforts, but Erin blamed herself for every misstep, and that made her performance worse. Erin had been quieter than usual that morning when they'd said goodbye to Caoimhe, Jane and Lily, and the difference in attitude between her and Caoimhe had been more pronounced than usual.

Even from this distance, Inés could see the tension in Erin's face as she set off, taking the first turn too quickly. Her pacing was off from the get-go, but Baby took the jumps in his stride and Inés started to feel more hopeful, grateful that Baby was looking after *her* baby so well. After the first few jumps were manoeuvred, Erin started to attack the fences and picked up the pace, barely pausing in the air over each jump. If they could get the water jump right and finish on a high note, Erin would come out confident tomorrow.

A subdued *ooooh* went around the onlookers as Erin took the water jump wrong and Baby landed a foot in the water. 'Four faults!' a disembodied voice cried over the tannoy.

Inés gasped, for a split second feeling her heart leap in her throat as she worried they would take a tumble or Baby would injure himself, but they landed without mishap and finished the course, albeit more slowly than they otherwise would have. Still, Inés thought Erin would have done well enough to keep her in the running for tomorrow. As Erin trotted out of the ring, Inés went down to join her, passing Elizabeth and Maria on the way. Like their children, they'd been joined at the hip all morning.

'A shame, that mistake on the water jump,' Elizabeth said sympathetically. Inés smiled tightly as Maria made a commiserating noise even though her eyes glittered with spite. 'Poor Erin. Has she been neglecting her practice, do you think? Chelsea has given it her all this year, and it's certainly paying off.'

'Erin has worked very hard,' Inés said firmly, 'and I'm proud of her. She's definitely still in the running for the team.'

'I do hope it doesn't end up being a competition between her and Ben for the final place,' Elizabeth sighed. 'It would be so awful if the competition ruined their friendship.'

Inés wondered how Elizabeth had managed to get the impression that Erin and Ben had any liking for each other, and decided it wasn't helpful to put her straight. Instead, she smiled again and carried on, ignoring Maria. She refused to waste her energy on the woman, reminding herself that Maria must be deeply unhappy to be so petty at every available opportunity.

As she reached the stables where Erin was rubbing down Million Dollar Baby, she saw Jack coming the other way. She hadn't spoken to him since turning down his offer of lunch the day before, and was relieved he seemed to have given up, as there'd been no more messages or missed calls.

'Good morning, Jack,' she said as he approached,

aiming for breezy politeness. Jack stopped in his tracks, gave her a pained look that was half anger, half hurt, and turned round to retreat back the way he'd come. Inés shook her head in bemusement.

Erin's mouth was set in a grim line as her mother approached. Before Inés could speak, she said, not looking at her as she brushed Baby down: 'I held for too long over the water jump.'

'You righted yourself; it could have been a lot worse. You're still in, darling. You should be pleased.'

Erin didn't answer, and Inés helped her finish up in silence. The groom came to take Baby, and after giving her horse a pat, briefly laying her head on his neck, Erin kissed him and told him she loved him anyway. They walked back to the hotel.

Inés checked her watch. It was past lunchtime, and with Erin obviously distressed, Inés decided to let Kent know she wouldn't be able to meet. She'd been looking forward to seeing him, but there was always another time for Kent. At some point between receiving the flowers and now, Inés realised she'd accepted his offer of a date, even if she hadn't let him know yet.

'Would you prefer to go to lunch or eat in our room or round the pool?' Inés asked. Erin shrugged.

'Don't take this the wrong way, mum, but can I take something to my room? I want to be on my own and get my head straight for tomorrow.'

Erin indeed disappeared into her room, and Inés knew pushing her to talk wouldn't help. Instead, she texted Kent to let him know she'd meet him downstairs for lunch. He messaged back almost immediately.

Great, be there in thirty minutes.

When her phone buzzed with another text a few moments later, Inés assumed it would be Kent again. Instead, Jack's name flashed up on the screen and Inés groaned.

I was really hurt by the way you dismissed me yesterday.
As though nothing had happened between us.
I think we should talk this out.

Inés pressed a hand to her head, rubbing her temple. She'd dealt with clingy and pushy men before, but this was bizarre. She left the message unopened and went to get changed for her brief lunch with Kent, choosing a white sundress, strappy sandals and delicate diamond studs. Light, but classy. Then she lightly tonged her hair and added a slick of Chanel's latest nude lipstick before grabbing her handbag.

She popped her head into Erin's room to find her lying on the bed, reading.

'I'll be in the restaurant downstairs. Do you want anything?'

Erin shook her head. 'I've ordered. Then I'm going to get a shower and a nap.'

Inés hesitated, feeling as though there was so much she should say, but unsure where to start. Instead, she crossed over to the bed, laid a light kiss on the crown of Erin's head and left her to it.

Kent was already waiting at a table for two near the wide glass windows that overlooked the beach. *A glorious view,* Inés thought, as she walked over to him. Kent looked her up and down with subtle but obvious admiration, and rose to kiss her cheek. 'Beautiful as ever. The sun suits you.'

'Thank you.' He looked pretty good himself; his skin was slightly tanned from the Spanish sun and it brought out the blue of his eyes and the silver flecks in his hair.

Kent pulled out a chair for Inés. 'So, how did our star jumper do today?' he asked. The way he said 'our' made Inés frown, reminding her uncomfortably of George and how she'd met Kent in the first place.

'Better than she realises,' she said with a sigh, picking up the menu. 'She's placed on the middle of the board; a good round tomorrow and she'll be in. But she's such a perfectionist that I can tell she's terribly disappointed with herself. It holds her back. She's incredibly talented.'

'Where do you think that comes from?' Kent asked, seeming genuinely interested. 'Just teenage angst, perhaps?'

'Well, she's the oldest of five, and I think she's a typical oldest child – her anxiety came on after George died. It's to be expected, of course, but she won't talk about it, so I'm unsure how to best address it.'

The waiter came over and Inés ordered a chicken salad

and fruit tart with a white wine spritzer, while Kent went for steak. 'Really? This time of day?' Inés laughed.

Kent shrugged. 'I skipped breakfast – I was up too late drinking with my new clients; you know how it goes. And I won't eat on the plane, I can't stand their food.'

'You always had an appetite when you used to come round for dinner,' Inés mused, flashing back to the last time Kent had come for dinner with her and George, bringing his latest date with him. Inés wondered what had happened to her and how long she'd lasted. There'd been a long line of often younger, adoring women on Kent's arm, but none seemed to stay.

'Speaking of which,' Kent said, his hand lightly brushing hers over the table, 'I take it you got my invitation along with the flowers?'

'I did. The flowers were beautiful.'

'And the invitation?' There was a slight edge to his voice – maybe Kent was anxious she'd reject him.

Inés smiled, holding his gaze. 'I'd love to go for dinner once we're back home and settled,' she said.

Kent's mouth broke into a broad grin and he playfully slapped his thigh, like the Texan he was. 'Best news I've had all trip.'

'Better than your business deal?'

'The deal is a close second,' he admitted. Inés laughed and took a sip of her drink, holding his eyes over the rim of her glass. Kent's gaze dropped seductively to her mouth, but then he looked over her shoulder and frowned. 'Do you know that guy? He doesn't look happy.'

Inés looked behind her, somehow already knowing who Kent was referring to.

Jack stood glaring, near the entrance of the restaurant. He caught Inés' eye and shook his head in outrage. For a moment she thought he was going to come over and cause a scene, but instead he turned on his heel and stormed off. Inés breathed a sigh of relief as she turned back round. She was going to have to talk to him; this was getting out of hand. There was no reason for Jack to be in her hotel – he must have come looking for her.

'Who on earth was that?'

Feeling slightly embarrassed, Inés explained briefly. 'He's one of the show officials. We had a sort of … casual date … two nights ago, and he hasn't taken that I don't want to see him again very well.'

Inés had half expected Kent to laugh and say something disparaging about Jack. Instead, his face momentarily darkened, and rage flashed in his eyes. The look was gone, replaced by a look of curiosity mixed with concern so suddenly, Ines wondered if she was mistaken.

'That was creepy; him standing there, glaring at you.'

'Nothing I can't handle,' Inés said lightly, 'but it is becoming a nuisance.'

'Would you like me to have a man-to-man talk with this guy?' Kent's display of protection excited Inés, but she was too proud to let someone else fight her battles, no matter how alluring the gesture was.

'Oh no. Like I said, I can handle the likes of him.'

Kent took her hand fully, stroking her palm with his

thumb. 'I get it.' His gaze was almost hypnotic. 'I can't imagine any man wanting to let you go.'

The waiter arrived with their food and Kent sat back, giving her hand a squeeze before letting it go. Her skin tingled where he'd touched her. Feeling disconcerted, Inés picked up her fork and turned her attention to her food.

Kent took a long swig of his wine. 'So,' he said with a nonchalance that was a touch too practised, 'should I be jealous?'

'Jealous?' Inés teased. 'Of Jack?'

'You're obviously in demand.' Kent was smiling but there was a slight edge to his voice, and Inés suddenly wasn't sure whether she should be flattered or annoyed. The attention was nice, but she was starting to feel hemmed in. Perhaps she'd been single and independent too long.

Or perhaps Jack's behaviour was unsettling her more than she wanted to admit.

'Erin said the same,' Inés grinned, trying to keep the conversation superficial. 'But I only have to deal with Jack for the next few days, thank God, and then we'll be home.'

Kent held her gaze and smiled. 'Well, if you change your mind, I'd be happy to be your personal bodyguard.'

'What are the perks?' she laughed, glad to have got past an awkward moment.

'Oh, let me think, how does complete and utter adoration sound?'

'I think I can live with that!'

They finished lunch, chatting amicably about Kent's business dealings and Inés' work and goings on at the yard, before Kent announced he had to go and get ready to catch his plane. Inés walked him to the foyer entrance and he kissed her lightly before heading off down the ramp. Inés thought she saw a man in the distance over by the beach, watching them, and wondered if it was Jack, but then the man walked out of sight. Shaking her head at her jumpiness, Inés went back up to her room.

The expected message appeared as she stepped out of the lift and on to the floor of her suite. It was Jack, of course.

> *So that's why you didn't want to do lunch with me.*
> *I should have known.*
> *Fast mover, aren't you?*

With an exasperated sigh, Inés dialled his number. This was getting beyond a joke. As soon as she heard the line connect, she spoke before he had a chance to say anything. 'What's this about, Jack? Why were you at my hotel?'

'I wanted to see you.' He sounded like a petulant child, and Inés wondered how she could ever have found him attractive.

'You've been sending me nasty messages. Why on earth would I want to see you?' she asked bluntly. The time for tiptoeing around this was over. He'd crossed the line from clingy date to potential stalker, and she wasn't going to have her trip ruined by a bad fling.

'Frankly, Inés,' he said haughtily, 'I'm surprised at your behaviour. It doesn't look dignified, you know, spending the night with me one minute and going out on a lunch date with another guy the next. Don't be surprised if people talk.'

Inés bristled with indignation. *How dare he?*

'This isn't the nineteen fifties, Jack,' she snapped. 'I doubt anyone would care. And not that it's any of your business, but I was having lunch with an old family friend. I certainly don't need anyone's permission, least of all yours. This has to stop. Your behaviour is bordering on harassment.'

'Harassment? Don't flatter yourself!' Jack sneered, although she thought she detected a hint of nervousness in his voice. She'd be within her rights to report it if this carried on. Then he said something she wasn't expecting.

'You really are a piece of work, Inés. You should think before you treat people like this – especially when you have a daughter currently competing in a competition *I* oversee.'

Inés quieted. Surely, no matter how hurt his pride, he wouldn't use his influence to jeopardise Erin's chances? Surely he wouldn't be *that* unethical?

'Don't you dare threaten me,' she barked, shaking with anger. She immediately wished she hadn't shown her feelings as he laughed mockingly.

'I can do what I want, Inés. Wish Erin good luck for me, won't you?' He cut the call, leaving Inés standing with the phone in her hand, feeling impotent with fury. She took a few deep breaths before entering her suite, not wanting to give Erin any inclination that something was wrong; the girl was anxious enough.

A rash decision that should have resulted in nothing more than a fun holiday fling was turning into a nightmare, and Inés would never forgive herself if her recklessness affected her daughter's chances. *Surely there was no way Jack had that sort of power?*

Squaring her shoulders, Inés took a breath. She went to spend the remainder of the day with Erin.

Chapter Fourteen

Early the next morning, Erin lay in bed staring at the ceiling. She'd been awake for hours, going over and over how best to attack today's course in her head. She had to go clear today if she was going to make the team, and no matter how much her mother assured her that she stood as much of a chance as any of them, Erin couldn't believe it. She kept seeing Chelsea and Ben's sneering faces and cringing inside. It shouldn't matter – *they* shouldn't matter, she told herself firmly.

Her mother's relentless encouragement wasn't helping, either – Erin couldn't share the faith her mother had in her. She also knew that no matter how much she'd try to hide it, Inés would be sorely disappointed if she didn't make the team.

Sometimes, when her nerves were this bad, Erin wondered if it would be better to stop show jumping and let Caoimhe be the sporty one – she could take pressure in her stride. Caoimhe only cared about winning and didn't care about losing, and that was Erin's downfall; she cared about winning and losing. Erin was sure she'd been like that herself, when she was younger, but something along the way had changed. Her fear of failure started to take over her competitive spirit.

Especially when her dad had died.

Erin closed her eyes against the old but still painful feelings of grief that threatened to wash over her and took a few deep breaths. She could hear the birds singing outside her window and Inés moving around in the next bedroom. It was time to get up. Willing the nausea that churned in her tummy to settle down, Erin got out of bed and started to get ready for the day ahead.

A few hours later, she was walking Baby around in the practice ring, trying to ignore Chelsea, who kept throwing her disdainful glances. 'What's her problem?' she muttered under her breath to her mother, who shook her head.

'I'd say it's teenage rivalry, but her mother, Maria, is exactly the same towards me. It's jealousy, darling, ignore them. Rising above it will irritate them more than anything else.'

What on earth could Chelsea be jealous of? thought Erin. She was as beautiful as her mother and in a good position on the scoreboard – she literally had it all. Unless Chelsea had a spectacularly bad round today, she'd definitely make the British team. *That in itself was enough to put anyone off competing.* Erin shuddered at the idea of spending more time with Chelsea at the upcoming international events.

Inés seemed off today too, glancing around as though looking for someone. *Probably Jack.* Inés hadn't said anything, but her phone had been buzzing all morning while they'd been getting ready, and judging by the way her mother had tightened her lips and turned her phone off before tossing it into her bag, it was someone she didn't want to speak to. They'd seen Jack from a distance a few times, but he hadn't come over to them and Inés seemed to be deliberately not looking in his direction. Erin wished she knew what was going on, but it would be pointless to ask.

They watched as Ben de Bohun was called in for his round. He looked pale as he cantered around the arena, and Erin wondered if he was ill. *It couldn't be nerves.* She'd never known him to be anything but supremely confident in himself, whether it was justified or not.

It wasn't a great round, even though Chelsea ran over to coo at Ben as he trotted into the practice ring. He looked conceited by her attention, and Erin watched as Ben handed his horse over to the groom without giving him so much as a pat and then went off with Chelsea, their heads together. Chelsea was giggling.

'Those two are up to something,' Inés murmured. 'I wonder what? And that was an unusually sloppy round.'

'Perhaps he's distracted by Chelsea,' Erin offered.

Inés shrugged. 'Maybe. But let's forget them; you'll be called soon. How are you feeling?' Inés' eyes searched her daughter's face.

Erin forced a smile, but she could tell her mother wasn't convinced. 'I'm as ready as I'll ever be,' she said, trying to ignore the churning in her stomach. When her name was called, the churning turned into a flutter of panic.

She tried to concentrate on the feeling of Baby underneath her, and stay in the moment, but her mind and thoughts felt scattered and she couldn't focus. For some reason, her father's face flashed in front of her and she felt a stab of grief, remembering his voice urging her on as though it were yesterday and she was still competing in the under-twelves.

At the same time, the grief spurred her on, and she felt a renewed focus as they set off. She and Baby moved as one around the course, and as if out of nowhere her pacing was perfect and Baby flew over the jumps like an absolute dream. They finished the round and Erin looked at the scoreboard with a huge grin on her face, already knowing what she'd see.

She trotted back over to Inés, to see her mother beaming with pride, with an 'I told you that you could do it' look on her face. Erin loved how her mother managed to be both glowing with pride when she did well, and yet supportive when she didn't, refusing to let her disappointment show.

'Three places up the scoreboard,' Inés said with a nod. 'Do that again this afternoon and you're definitely in.'

'It's not just about scores,' Erin reminded her. Although each round was scored by speed and the number of faults, there were other factors the team selectors would take into account when selecting riders. The health of the horse, the experience of horse and rider in the preceding months, and whether the rider was willing to take direction from the team manager all came into play when the decisions were made. But good scores mattered, and Erin was glad that was another round down, at least.

She tried not to think about the fact that this afternoon's round would be her last chance, or the pressure would start piling up again.

Chapter Fifteen

'Thank you, Father,' Alice said politely, showing the priest out. It had taken her all afternoon to get rid of him. *He'd have been happy to sit in the kitchen drinking whiskey and reminiscing with her about Ireland until the sun had gone down,* Alice thought, but she needed him gone before the twins got home from school.

She shut the door behind him and walked slowly around the house. She hadn't wanted to admit it to Father Seamus, but the house didn't feel any different to her, despite his mumbling and sprinkling of holy water in the corners of each room. Still, she supposed she wouldn't know until night fell, because that was when she heard the footsteps. Perhaps she *was* going crazy. Either that or her suspicions were right; the ghost was George, and he wasn't at rest.

Tutting loudly, Alice went into the kitchen to check the casserole she'd put in the slow cooker that morning. It was bubbling nicely and she turned it off after taking a deep and appreciative sniff. She didn't get the chance to cook for her family much anymore, and although she'd never have admitted it to Inés, she was enjoying it.

The priest had left just in time; the front door burst

open and the twins tumbled in, chattering loudly between themselves. They saw Alice and hugged her simultaneously, their movement coordinated.

'Hey, granny.'

'School was great.'

'What's for dinner?'

'It smells great.'

'We've invited Charlie. Is that okay?'

'Hope you've made enough.'

They ran upstairs to get changed out of their school uniforms before Alice had the chance to answer their quick-fire questions. She was getting the plates out of the dishwasher when the doorbell rang. Alice let Charlie in, giving him a big smile. She had a soft spot for the lad from next door. As much as she loved her granddaughters, she'd have liked a grandson as well, but Inés and George's genes together had seemed intent on producing girls. Charlie fitted in well with the Cullen family. No doubt their busy, bustling household helped assuage his loneliness, with a father who, by the sound of things, didn't have much time for his son.

'Hey, Alice. Whatever that is, it smells delicious.'

'Mince and dumplings,' Alice said with an indulgent smile. 'Come on in.'

Watching the three of them tuck in, and then ask for seconds, gave Alice a warm glow of pride. Inés hated stews and anything she considered 'old-fashioned food,' although, as Alice never missed the chance to remind her, she'd grown up on good, hearty Irish stews and they'd never done her any harm. Sometimes, Alice wondered if Inés wasn't too modern for her own good. *She'd never been interested in traditional dancing, either,* she thought with a sigh, no matter how many Saturday mornings Alice had dragged her daughter to classes as a child.

'Are you coming on Skype with us, granny?' Imogen asked as she put down her spoon and patted her belly. 'We're going to talk to Nanny Jane, Caoimhe and Lily.'

'That sounds nice,' Alice said dubiously, not wanting to admit she didn't know what Skype was. *What on earth was wrong with the telephone?*

'I'll show you how to set it up if you want,' Charlie said kindly, clearly guessing her thoughts. 'Then you can see them whenever you want.'

'Granny doesn't have a laptop,' Fiadh and Imogen said simultaneously.

He set the twins' laptop up while they loaded the dishwasher and Alice poured herself a whiskey. It was only her third – well, maybe fourth – of the day, but it was nice to help herself to a drink without Inés, Jane or Erin watching her with disapproval. It wasn't as though she drank vodka or gin like an alcoholic. This was whiskey; *practically medicine, for goodness' sake!*

Caoimhe's face appeared on the screen, her features slightly distorted by the smudged lens. 'Hi guys!' she said loudly, her ponytail bouncing around her shoulders.

She was becoming a beautiful young woman; Alice thought she resembled herself as a teenage girl. All the boys in her home village had wanted to take her out dancing. She sighed and sipped at her whiskey, listening to the girls and Charlie as they chatted away. Caoimhe was winning all her classes and was as cheerful as ever. Lily sat on Jane's lap, pulling faces at the camera.

'I miss you, granny,' she pouted. 'You'd have loved the museum. It was noisy, though.'

'Noisy?' Alice asked, puzzled. *Wasn't that the opposite of what a museum should be?*

'She set the alarms off,' Jane explained with a long-suffering air, 'because she insisted on trying to climb up one of the displays. They asked us to leave.'

'We had seen everything by then, anyway,' Caoimhe said, clearly holding back laughter.

Poor Jane looked exhausted and Lily was in her pyjamas, but Alice suspected no one would be going to sleep any time soon.

They said goodbye, and then the twins saw Charlie out and disappeared up to their room, leaving the house empty and quiet again. Alice hoped it would stay that way, and there were going to be no more bumps in the night. She took her drink and went to her bedroom, preparing for an early night. Three hours later, she was awakened by a creaking of the stairs and rustling noises. Swearing, she threw the duvet over her head and tried her best to get back to sleep.

Chapter Sixteen

Inés and Erin sat on the terrace having a cool drink, watching some of the other rounds. Inés was excited about Erin's improved performance that morning, but she also knew her daughter well enough to know she'd now be putting intense pressure on herself to repeat it. If she didn't make the team now, the loss would be much more bitter. It was a tough sport, deeply competitive and requiring a high level of bravery to fly around such difficult courses at the speeds they did. Erin was plucky, which worked in her favour, so the danger had never bothered her.

Turning to face the bar, watching people including officials coming and going, Inés spotted two of the selectors from the Irish team ordering drinks. She enjoyed watching the Irish team, and not just because she and George were both Irish born. There was something more down-to-earth and focused about the team, and they had a reputation for training hard and putting the win above all else. There was none of the nonsense she so often saw on other teams. Then she thought of her night with Jack and shifted uncomfortably in her chair. Inés didn't have many regrets, but that was quickly becoming one. She'd made a mistake in expecting him to be both liberal and mature enough to handle it, and instead his petty jealousy was becoming unnerving. *It was a shame the British team weren't more like the Irish*, she thought ruefully. They would certainly be much better in temperament for Erin.

That gave Inés an idea. She told Erin she was going to fetch them another fruit juice.

She propped her elbows on to the bar and looked round for a waiter, buying herself a few minutes before speaking. She thought about how to address the situation and what to say. Erin wanted to ride at the Europeans; it didn't necessarily have to be for the British team.

Go get it.

'How's it going this year?' she asked. The first man, whose name tag identified him as Ted, grimaced slightly. 'Not so bad,' he said gruffly. 'There's some good talent, but the standard isn't what it used to be.'

'We're always on the lookout for talent,' the other man jumped in, with a broad smile.

'Right,' Inés said casually. 'It might not sound like it, but I'm from Ireland.'

'Oh?' he said in surprise. 'Where in Ireland are you from? Why no accent?'

'Tralee. We moved to England when I was young,' she said. 'I lost it pretty quickly, but it sometimes appears if I lose my temper.'

Ted laughed. 'You thinking of trying out, then?'

Inés laughed along with him. 'Not quite. You might have noticed my daughter Erin this morning, on Million Dollar Baby? She did splendidly.'

Ted and Michael glanced over at Erin and Michael nodded in recognition. 'Yes, I saw her. Good jumper. Great horse, too. She's bound to make the team.'

'Oh, I expect so,' Inés said lightly.

'I've heard there's a lot of competition on the British team this year,' Ted countered bluntly. 'Have an Irish passport, does she, your daughter?'

Inés nodded nonchalantly. 'Well, keep us in mind, just in case,' he advised.

'Will do,' Inés said, then moved down the bar to catch the attention of the bartender. She returned to her table with two glasses of fresh pineapple juice.

'Who were they?' Erin asked.

'Selectors from the Irish team,' Inés said lightly, sipping at her drink. 'They were commenting on how good your round was.'

'Oh, that was nice of them,' Erin said, chewing her lip. 'I hope I can do the same this afternoon.'

'Give it your best shot, sweetheart, and don't let those two horrors distract you. They seem more interested in each other than the competition in any case, which might well work in our favour.'

'You mean Ben and Chelsea?'

'Who else?'

Erin smiled, but with less mirth than Inés was expecting. She was feeling the pressure.

Right on cue, Inés heard Elizabeth's voice behind her and turned to see her making her way over to the table next to them with Maria, who was complaining loudly about the service at her hotel. She stopped mid-flow when she saw Inés and Erin and gave them a smile that was more like a grimace.

'Hello, darling,' Elizabeth said gaily, bending down to kiss Inés' cheek and enveloping her in a haze of perfume so strong that it made Inés cough. Underneath the heavy floral and musk tones, Inés caught the scent of alcohol. Elizabeth was getting worse, and Maria seemed to be a terrible influence. Not that she was a heavy drinker, as far as Inés knew, but she certainly seemed to encourage Elizabeth, no doubt because it helped keep her new friend pliable.

'Hello, Elizabeth. Final round's coming up,' Inés said.

Elizabeth nodded and beamed at Erin. 'You were excellent this morning, dear,' she said. Erin's expression brightened as she thanked her.

Maria narrowed her eyes like a cat. 'Yes, you must have had a run of good luck this morning; much better than your usual standard.'

Erin visibly deflated in her chair. Inés' protective, maternal instinct kicked in and she'd opened her mouth to respond to Maria when she saw Jack approaching, a big smile on his face.

Inés raised an eyebrow at Erin instead. 'Shall we go?'

'There was no offence meant,' Maria said silkily.

Inés shook her head, tired of this nonsense. 'Honestly, Maria, I don't believe that for one minute.'

As she got up to go, Jack arrived, and Inés realised his smile hadn't been for her. Instead, he made a great show of embracing Maria, holding her for far longer than appropriate while flashing Inés an oddly triumphant look.

Really? He's trying to make me jealous? Inés rolled her eyes and walked away.

'Well, that was fun,' Erin said morosely.

'Don't let them get to you,' Inés said firmly. 'A place on the team is well within your sights. That's why she's being mean; she doesn't want you to get on in place of Chelsea or Ben. This is why Molly keeps Tristan as far away from them as possible.'

'Yes, but Tristan's brilliant,' Erin said with a sigh.

'That doesn't mean their words don't affect him any less.'

As the afternoon went on and they waited for her to be called, Inés could see Erin withdrawing and becoming more and more tense. When Ben and Chelsea returned, and Ben had a great round in spite of the fact he seemed more interested in Chelsea than in competing, Inés decided that things were going to be tight, but for Erin's sake she needed to remain positive. A few times she saw Jack glaring, or alternatively smirking, at her but she did her best to let it go over her head, although she was worried now about his influence as a team selector. He was an official, after all, and they took the sport seriously. *Surely he wouldn't be so petty as to influence Erin's chances?*

Finally, it was Erin's last round. Inés watched her trot into the ring on Baby and saw the telltale creases of worry between her eyes. As soon as they set off, Inés knew it wasn't going to be a repeat of the morning. Her speed and timing was off, and she knocked down a pole on one of the jumps, and then Baby refused the water jump, which was a major fault. Erin came out of the ring looking as though she was holding back tears.

'You're not out yet,' Inés assured her. 'One bad round isn't enough to knock you out. You're an asset to that team, and they'll see it, I'm sure.' But even as Inés spoke she felt a lurch in her stomach, and when the selection was called and Erin hadn't made the team, Inés was disappointed but not wholly surprised. It was the first time Erin hadn't made it on to a team.

Erin looked devastated. She didn't speak on the way back to the hotel at all, and when they got into their suite, she stormed into her bedroom.

'Can I get you anything?' Inés called.

'Leave me alone, mum,' Erin shouted tearfully, slamming the bedroom door shut behind her.

Inés placed her bag down on the counter and started to make herself a drink. She'd give Erin a while, and then go and try to comfort her. Her phone buzzed in her bag and she reached for it, expecting it to be either Jane or possibly Kent, but her heart sank when she saw a message from Jack. She hoped he didn't have the audacity to gloat over Erin not making the team.

But it was worse. She scrolled through his message, hardly able to believe her eyes.

Shame your girl didn't make the team today.
Perhaps you shouldn't have been such a bitch to

me and things may have been different. Rejection hurts, doesn't it?

Inés sucked in a sharp breath, flooding with anger and burning with injustice on behalf of her daughter. *No,* she thought determinedly, *I'm not going to let him do this to us.*

Whether he'd influenced Erin's chances or was merely gloating, Inés didn't know, but it certainly seemed like he was taking credit for her exclusion. Whatever his intentions, Jack's behaviour was unforgivable. *To compromise his integrity to the sport because he felt rejected by me?* It was as childish as it was cruel. There was no way Inés was going to let him get away with it and fly home with her tail between her legs.

But before she could think about any of that, she needed to go and comfort her eldest.

Chapter Seventeen

Erin heard the door open and roughly wiped the tears away from her cheeks, even though she knew her mother would think no less of her for crying. She kept seeing the sneering faces of Ben, Chelsea and Maria, and thinking of the satisfaction her tears would give them. She sat up, only to crumple into tears again when she looked into her mother's eyes. 'I'm okay, Mum,' she said fiercely. Inés nodded and waited, patiently, for Erin to speak.

'I don't know what's wrong with me sometimes,' she said after a long silence, rubbing at her wet cheeks. 'It's like, I know I can do better, but I freeze up and everything goes wrong. As soon as I make one mistake I panic, and it gets worse. After I did so well this morning, instead of it giving me confidence, I felt under even more pressure. It's so stupid. I'm stupid,' she mumbled, feeling a wave of shame.

Inés took her hand gently, but her voice was firm. 'Erin, don't speak about yourself like that. You're not stupid at all; far from it in fact. No one can win everything.'

'Caoimhe does,' Erin grumbled, feeling a twinge of resentment against her younger sister.

'Taekwondo is a very different sport,' Inés said evenly.

'This isn't about a lack of talent, Erin, it's about your nerves. Do you know where it comes from?'

Erin shook her head glumly, though a voice in her mind whispered to her that she did in fact have a good idea where her anxiety came from. It went a lot deeper than worrying about how she looked to Ben and Chelsea.

'You don't have to carry on competing if you don't want to, love,' Inés said softly. 'There's no pressure from me; your well-being is more important than a few trophies.'

Erin thought for a moment. It sounded tempting; the idea of giving up competing and riding purely for pleasure again. Never again would she have to worry about last-minute nerves ruining her performance, or the feeling that she was letting everyone down. It would make life so much easier … yet something in her rebelled at the thought of giving up. She might be anxious, frightened, even self-sabotaging at times, but she wasn't a quitter. Her mother hadn't raised her to ever give up. *Ever.* She had more backbone, and besides there were times when she loved competing, when she had a good round and she and Baby moved like they were one – there was no feeling like it. When Erin was younger, it had felt like that, regardless of whether she had won or not.

She said as much to her mother, who nodded in agreement, then hesitated before she spoke. 'Erin, I put it down to you getting older – teenage hormones and all that, but it's more than that isn't it? This is about your father.'

Erin was startled and her mouth opened in an 'oh' of surprise. But she didn't deny it, because Inés was right.

She nodded, looking down at her hands which she'd been twisting together in her lap without being aware of the movement; a sure sign of her anxiety.

'I feel like I'm letting him down,' she said in a rush, fresh tears stinging her eyes. 'Sometimes, when I do well, like this morning, I can see him there, smiling at me like he used to. He was so proud of me, do you remember? He came to every show. He used to say I was his little show-jumping superstar and I was going to break world records, and I believed him.' She took a deep breath, choking back sobs as she continued. 'So now, when I don't do so well, I can't help thinking about how disappointed he'd be in me, and I can almost see him there, looking sad because I've let him down, and then I get even more nervous and the round goes even more badly. I want to feel like I did when he was still here.' She stopped, her shoulders heaving, and Inés pulled her into a tight embrace and let her cry out four years of grief and anxiety.

It went on for a long time. By the time Erin pulled her head away, Inés' shirt was wet with tears and Erin's eyes were swollen. 'I've ruined your shirt,' she mumbled apologetically.

'It'll wash,' Inés said practically. Her face was etched with concern. 'Erin, I suspected something like this might be going on, but never how deeply this was getting to you. Why didn't you come to me?'

Erin shrugged. 'I don't know. I suppose I was embarrassed. I didn't want to upset you.'

Inés shook her head and stroked Erin's hair.

'Sweetheart, I'm your mother, it's what I'm here for. I know you're the oldest and you look out for your sisters, but you don't have to shoulder my burdens too, love. I'm always on your side. I'm here for you regardless of what's happening. Always.'

'I know.' Erin exhaled heavily, realising she felt lighter now, and raw, as though someone had scrubbed her out from the inside. 'I wish I had now.'

'You do know it's not true?' Inés said gently. 'George would never have been disappointed in you, even if you failed every round.' A smile creased Inés' face. 'Well, maybe not *every* round.'

Erin emitted a giggle then sniffed hard and rubbed at her eyes.

'He'd have been every bit as proud of you for having the guts to come out here and do it. I know I am.'

Erin heard the ring of truth in her words, and smiled as she thought back to her memories of her father, knowing that Inés was right. 'I've let it build up in my head, haven't I?'

'It sounds that way, sweetheart.'

'The thing is,' Erin began and hesitated, not wanting to cause any trouble, 'I did try to talk about it to granny, last year. But…'

Inés sighed. 'What did she say?'

'Her usual stuff about his spirit not being at rest. I knew it was silly, but I couldn't get the idea out of my head that he really was there, watching every time I didn't do well. Every time I failed.'

'My bloody mother,' Inés grumbled. 'I have to put my foot down about this.'

But she hadn't said it was a load of rubbish like she usually did. Maybe there was something in what granny said. Inés had definitely been on edge recently.

'It sounds so silly now,' Erin commented.

Inés smiled wryly. 'That's what happens when you keep things to yourself; they get bigger and scarier. I'm glad you've finally told me.'

'Me too.' She felt as though she'd been relieved of a burden she'd been carrying for so long she'd forgotten how to be without it. There was one more thing…

'It's a bit late though, isn't it? I'm off the team now.'

Inés opened her mouth as if to reply and then stopped.

Erin frowned. 'What is it?'

'I have a suggestion,' Inés said slowly. 'It's entirely up to you. I don't want you to feel under any pressure.'

'No. Go on, what?' Erin asked her mother, intrigued by her words.

'Well, you have an Irish passport.'

For a moment, Erin stared at Inés, wondering what on earth she was talking about. Then it dawned on her. 'You mean … try out for the Irish team?'

'I was speaking to their selectors at the bar earlier. They seemed … receptive. They saw your performance this morning and were impressed.'

Erin thought about it, then her face burst into a wide smile. 'That would make dad so proud!'

'Yes,' Inés said hesitantly, 'but the last thing I want is

you putting more pressure on yourself. Your father would be as proud, regardless. And as harsh as it sounds, he isn't here, love. This has to be about what *you* want, not your father, me, or anyone else.'

'I know what I want,' Erin said quietly. 'And I can't believe how much better I feel for finally opening up about it all. Thanks, mum.'

They shared a smile. Erin stretched her legs out in front of her and said: 'Can we order food? I'm starving.'

Inés laughed. 'That's more like it. Do you want to go out or get room service?'

'Do you mind if we stay here? My eyes feel puffy.'

'Of course not. In fact, it sounds great. Let's order and eat out on the balcony; it's a beautiful evening.'

Erin had a shower and changed into shorts and a vest and then joined her mother out on the balcony. The sound of grasshoppers and a heavy scent of camellias, set against the mellow evening air and stunning view of the beach, made Erin feel more relaxed than she had in months, maybe even years. She couldn't put her finger on it, but her emotional outburst seemed to have shifted something within her.

When her mother's phone rang, she saw Inés' mouth tighten and wondered what was going on. Although she knew Inés wouldn't tell her, Erin wasn't blind and could see that someone – most likely that weirdo Jack who kept glaring at her everywhere she went – was bothering her. But Inés smiled and answered the phone, mouthing 'Caoimhe' at her.

It came as no surprise that Caoimhe had won the European Championships for her age group and would be coming home with a new medal, but Erin didn't feel as envious as she'd expected. Instead, she took the phone and wished her sister congratulations, grinning as Caoimhe gave her a moment-by-moment rundown of the competition. Erin told her she hadn't made the team. And Erin didn't mind that she hadn't.

'I am so sorry to hear that, Erin,' Caoimhe said.

'I'm not,' Erin laughed. 'I feel really good about it.'

Lily came on the line, sounding sleepy, after which Erin passed the phone back to Inés so she could speak to Jane. By the time Inés put the phone down she was shaking her head in exasperation.

'What's Lily done now?' Erin asked.

'Oh, she's been running rings around Jane all day. The poor woman sounds exhausted. We'll have to think of a treat for her. I knew I should have kept Lily here.'

'Granny says Lily's a changeling, left by the fairies.'

'Yes,' Inés said drily, 'she would, wouldn't she? She may be right!' They burst out laughing.

Their food arrived and they ate while watching the sun go down, bleeding out over the sky and turning the ocean orange. The grasshoppers had quietened and a lazy heat seemed to linger over everything, making Erin feel drowsy. She yawned heavily.

'Do you mind if I get an early night, mum?'

'Not at all. I'm going to sit out here and read.'

Erin kissed her on the cheek and then, before she went

back inside, she turned and said over her shoulder, almost nonchalantly: 'I've decided. I'm going to try out for the Irish team.'

'Oh, that's nice,' Inés said casually, giving her an encouraging nod. Erin went into the suite, and she was sure she heard Inés mumble under her breath, in a voice filled with satisfaction: 'That's my girl.'

Chapter Eighteen

That's my girl, Inés thought, catching Erin's eye as Million Dollar Baby trotted back into the training area, his step jaunty as though he was also proud of their performance.

'Well done,' Inés said, unable to contain her pride as Erin swung down from Baby's back. The scoreboard said it all; Erin was leading after her second round of the day. In a few hours, the names would be called, and although Inés didn't want to seem too certain in case Erin's hopes were crushed again, she'd have put money on her making the Irish team.

After taking Baby to the stables and getting changed, Inés and Erin went up to the show terrace, reserved for VIPs. Even the sight of Maria and Elizabeth at their usual table with a bottle of wine open in front of them couldn't dampen their happy mood.

'Well done, Reenie,' Elizabeth hiccupped, her voice far too loud across the terrace. 'You've done really well today. You were like lightning around that course.'

'Thank you,' Erin said sincerely, obviously too happy to correct Elizabeth's version of her name. Even if for some bizarre reason Erin didn't make the Irish team, she'd be overjoyed just on the strength of her performance.

'Of course, it's a shame you won't be able to compete with Ben. He'll miss you on the team, I'm sure.'

Inés raised an eyebrow, but seeing that Elizabeth looked completely sincere, she smiled. Erin widened her eyes innocently. 'I'll miss him, too. But I think he's pre-occupied enough by Chelsea. I'm sure they can keep each other company,' she said sweetly.

Inés coughed into her drink while Maria glared and Elizabeth looked faintly bemused. 'Yes,' she said, 'it's so nice to see everyone getting on, isn't it, Maria?'

Maria ignored Elizabeth and gave Erin a haughty look. 'You did do fairly well. Still, I suppose the pressure is off now the team has been called.'

'Yes, I suppose you're right,' Inés said, knowing her agreement would baffle her. She angled herself away from Maria and towards Erin, ignoring the other woman now. If Erin made the Irish team, neither she nor Inés would have to deal with her bullshit. Maria was a snob and difficult to get along with, but this year she was truly excelling herself in the bitch stakes and frankly Inés had had enough. She couldn't wait to get home.

To see Kent? a voice in her mind whispered.

Inés couldn't deny that his attention was flattering. Although a lingering sense of guilt over George remained, the conversation with Erin last night had released some ghosts for Inés, too. Holding on to George was serving no one, not herself or the children. She'd always love him, of course she would, but her friends were right, she couldn't stay in limbo forever.

Thinking about the past reminded Inés that the tax document was still bothering her. It was likely a blip, something her accountants would no doubt have sorted out by the time she returned home, but it had still unsettled her, bringing up old fears. *What if Kent were wrong? What if George had been driven to the edge by his failures?*

Inés shuddered, feeling momentarily cold, as though a shadow had passed over her. *It's nothing,* she told herself fiercely, *you're spooking yourself.* Alice's silly talk about intruders and ghosts had got to her, that was all. She'd have to have a word with her mother about that when she was home, because it had clearly affected Erin, too.

'Mum!' Erin said excitedly, thankfully pulling Inés out of her reverie. 'They're about to call the Irish team.'

Inés took Erin's hand under the table, her eyes fixed firmly on the selection screen. When Erin's name was the first to be announced, her daughter whooped with joy, nearly knocking their drinks over as she hugged Inés. 'Thank you, mum,' she said tearfully as she pulled away.

'For what? You did it, sweetheart.'

'It was your idea!' Erin could barely sit still, bouncing in her seat with glee.

'Oh, Reenie, I'm so, so, pleased for you,' Elizabeth gushed from the next table, slurring the end of her words. Even Maria offered a forced smile.

'Come on,' Inés said, standing up. 'Let's go and celebrate with the rest of the team: get to know them better.'

As they went to leave the terrace, they spotted Ben and Chelsea making their way over to their mothers' table. Ben had his arm around Chelsea and she had her head on his shoulder. They were weaving between tables, their gait unsteady. Ben had a silly, unfocused grin on his face, while Chelsea's usually tanned face had paled. As they got closer, Inés realised Ben was all but holding Chelsea up.

'Mum,' Erin whispered, sounding worried, 'I think they're drunk.'

Inés nodded, hardly able to believe the kids were in such an obvious state of intoxication. Two of the officials from the British team were over at the other side of the terrace, and were watching with disapproving glares. Maria jumped out of her seat as they approached, announcing in a loud voice that Inés had no doubt was for the officials' benefit: 'Darling, I told you to keep out of the heat! She's got sunstroke. Let's get you lying down, you poor thing.'

'S'not sunstroke,' Chelsea slurred, then giggled. 'Don't be such a square, mum.'

She threw up all over Maria's expensive white stilettos. Ben jumped out of the way to avoid the vomit, staggered and crashed into the nearest table, knocking glasses flying and landing in the lap of an elderly man who looked unfazed by the sudden appearance of a person on his lap.

'Ben!' Elizabeth shrieked, running over to help him to his feet, although she was clearly unsteady herself.

Inés took a pack of tissues out of her handbag and handed them to Maria as she stared with horror down at her shoes. 'Come on,' she said quietly, 'I'll help you get Chelsea back to the hotel.' As much as she disliked the pair of them, Inés had no wish to see them humiliated.

Maria ignored her and instead turned towards Elizabeth, her face screwed up with rage. 'This is your fault!'

Elizabeth blinked in confusion. 'Mine?'

'Yes. It's your son who has got my daughter into this state! Plying her with drink – no doubt trying to take advantage of her!'

Elizabeth gasped, looking shocked and hurt, while Ben grinned and hiccupped at the same time. 'Hardly,' he said. 'She's the one who got the stuff, not me.'

'Stuff?' Elizabeth asked, looking horrified.

'What's going on here?' It was Eric, the chef d'equipe, with a face like thunder. He was a fair-haired Yorkshireman and didn't stand for any nonsense. 'Like I don't have enough to do coordinating the team, without wasting time on this sort of behaviour.'

Maria grabbed Chelsea's arm and marched off with her, while Eric glared at a now sullen and silent Ben. Eric stormed off after Maria, and Inés went over to Elizabeth, who was by now looking utterly distraught.

'I'll walk you back to your hotel,' Inés offered, extending a hand. Nodding miserably, Elizabeth stood and took it, murmuring her thanks.

'Come on,' Erin said behind them, nudging Ben none too lightly in the ribs. 'You'd better come as well before you get into any more trouble.'

Back at their hotel, Ben disappeared into his room and

could soon be heard being sick, while Inés got Elizabeth a large glass of water and ordered some toast.

'What will happen now?' Elizabeth said with a sob. 'Will they get kicked off the team?'

'They may just get a dressing down.' Inés suspected that there was no way Ben and Chelsea would be allowed to represent Britain after this, but it wasn't the moment to tell Elizabeth.

Before they left, Elizabeth grabbed her arm, her eyes pleading. 'You won't say anything to Guy, will you?'

'No, Elizabeth, that's something you have to do.' Inés left with Erin, and for a few minutes on the way back to their suite, neither of them spoke.

'I felt sorry for her,' Erin said after a while.

'So did I,' said Inés with a sigh. 'You know, I'm incredibly lucky with you girls.'

'You don't know how Lily or the twins will turn out yet,' Erin said with a grin.

• • •

Later, as Inés was preparing to go down for an evening swim and Erin was curled up with her headphones, Inés got a call from reception to tell her there was a man downstairs who wanted to see her. Frowning, Inés made her way to the reception, wondering who it could possibly be. For a moment she wondered if it was Kent, and felt a small flutter in her tummy, but that made no sense; he'd gone home two days ago.

When she reached the foyer and saw Jack, she

immediately stiffened. She looked around for security, prepared to have him thrown out if he was going to start acting up. But then he approached her awkwardly, avoiding direct eye contact.

'What do you want?' Inés asked sharply.

'I've been sent by Eric,' he said, looking shamefaced. Inés suddenly realised exactly what was going on.

'Really? Why?'

Jack shuffled from one foot to the other. 'Ben and Chelsea have been thrown off the team,' he said eventually. 'It seems they were stoned. Chelsea bought some weed from a waiter. It's too public. They can't represent Britain after that shambles, especially at their age.'

Inés shook her head. She'd guessed they'd been drinking, which was bad enough as they were underage, but taking drugs at the qualifiers? Inés would be amazed if either of them were ever allowed to try out again.

'Poor Elizabeth,' she said softly. 'She'll be devastated. But why,' she asked more firmly, 'are you telling me this?'

'I'm sure you can guess.'

'No idea,' Inés said with smug abandon.

'Erin. She was very close to making the team, after all.'

Inés was quiet for a moment, letting Jack feel every moment of embarrassment. 'So,' she said, her voice tight with quiet outrage, 'you're coming begging now the team is low on numbers, after telling me you were going to ruin Erin's chances? Well, well.'

Jack looked horrified, glancing around the foyer to make sure no one had heard. 'I didn't mean that!' he hissed. 'I'm only one of the selectors. I don't make the decisions on my own.'

'No, but you argued against her, am I right? You're an idiot, Jack.'

Jack went red and looked down at the floor again while Inés shook her head in disgust. 'I'll consider it,' she said, thinking shrewdly, 'but I want a team meeting with the officials –including you.'

Jack looked panicked. 'Whatever for?'

'I have a few requests,' Inés said. 'These things should be done properly. You have to understand, we've made a commitment to the Irish team. We have to weigh up our options.'

'Of course,' Jack said, sounding resigned. 'I'll tell Eric. It'll probably be in the morning; I'll get a message to you.'

'Wonderful,' Inés said lightly. 'I'll see you tomorrow, Jack.'

She turned on her heel and walked away from him, a small smile on her face.

'Have a wonderful evening,' she called over her shoulder.

Chapter Nineteen

Inés waited to be shown into the meeting. She was glad she'd brought a smart blazer and trousers, because she intended to go into the room like a lawyer. Inés' natural sense of justice, not to mention her maternal instincts, had been roused by the way Erin had been treated, and she wasn't the sort of woman to take it lying down.

Of course, if Erin had wanted the place, Inés would have supported her. Her daughter's happiness came before vindicating herself, but Erin's response to the offer, when Inés had got back to the hotel room to tell her, had been to laugh. 'No way, mum,' she'd said. 'I'm not being the replacement for either of those two. I have a much better option now. The Irish team looks great, and it's a complete fresh start for me.' It was exactly what Inés had expected her to say.

A young woman with a severe blonde bob came out of the meeting room and introduced herself as Sophie. Inés walked in with her head held high and a smile. Sophie showed Inés to her seat at the middle of the long table. She glanced around the room and spoke a quick 'hello' to each member present. Eric was opposite her, with Jack to his right. Sophie took her seat next to Jack and opened her laptop to take notes. On the other side of Eric were two men and another woman. After introductions, they were revealed as show coordinators, and the young woman was the riders' well-being supervisor.

'I'm glad you could come in today, Mrs Cullen,' Eric began, in an oddly stiff and overly formal voice. 'This is merely a formality.'

'Thank you,' Inés murmured demurely, sitting down and looking around her expectantly. She couldn't help smiling. Jack, who was obviously on edge, seemed to be making himself as small as possible in his chair.

'Mrs Cullen,' Eric continued, 'I think you're aware why we have invited you here today, and we hope we can come to a formal agreement regarding Erin's place on the team.'

'Erin doesn't have a place on the British team,' Inés said.

'Not yet, but given certain recent events, we now have two open places on the team. We'd like to invite her to accept one.'

'Why do you want her now?' Inés asked bluntly. 'After all, you considered her unsuitable.'

Eric looked around the room for assistance on the matter. Jack avoided eye contact and so Eric continued: 'As you know,' he said pompously, 'these competitions are often tight and deciding who makes the cut often involves tough decisions, as I'm sure you can appreciate. Erin was close to being picked, which is why we're extending this offer now as our first choice to fill the gap left due to – certain unfortunate events.'

Inés suppressed a smirk at his diplomatic phrasing. 'Thank you,' she said with as much sincerity as she could muster. 'I'm glad you have noticed Erin's talent, and I'm sure that if things were different, we'd be thrilled to accept your offer. As it is, however, I'm afraid we must decline.'

Eric looked shocked, as Inés had expected he would. She looked over at Jack, who was carefully avoiding her gaze as well, and seemed interested in a picture of a peacock hanging on the wall opposite him.

'Decline? My dear, this is a most coveted position. Can I ask why?'

Inés wasn't surprised it hadn't occurred to Eric that they'd say no. He'd assume they'd jump at the chance, even though he probably knew about Erin's place with the Irish team. Of course, that now meant she was a direct competitor of theirs in the European Championships in a matter of weeks, and after her stellar performance yesterday, she had no doubt they were desperate to have her back on the British team, especially with Chelsea and Ben gone.

Inés held all the cards.

'Erin has secured a place on the Irish team,' she said. 'I'm sure you saw her amazing rounds for them yesterday.'

Eric inclined his head, acknowledging her words. 'Indeed, she displayed a great deal of bravery and talent yesterday, and I was impressed to see her out there again after her recent disappointment. That type of spirit is exactly what we need on the team. But Erin has always competed as a Brit. She represented England when she was younger. Surely our team is her natural home?' he said, a puzzled look on his face.

Inés gave him an apologetic smile. 'I'm afraid we still must decline, and for two reasons. Firstly, it wouldn't be morally acceptable to either Erin or myself to let the Irish team down at this stage.'

She let her words hang in the air as she eyed the chef d'equipe coolly, knowing he'd not be ignorant of the fact that their attempt to poach Erin back to their team was nothing short of unethical. He dropped his gaze from hers, cleared his throat as though embarrassed, and composed himself to ask: 'You said there were two reasons. Can I ask the second?'

'Of course.' Inés smiled over the table at Jack and saw a flicker of worry in his eyes as he caught her gaze. She took a beat, then began. 'I'm worried about the level of corruption that's befallen the association this year.'

There were gasps around the table, and Eric spluttered in surprise. Jack's eyes darted everywhere but at Inés.

'That's a serious accusation!' Eric thundered in annoyance. 'Would you be so kind as to explain?'

'Certainly,' Inés said briskly. 'I'm referring to the fact that a team selector threatened to sabotage Erin's chances because they held a personal grudge against me.'

The older man blinked a few times, and then shook his head with relief, as though he'd expected something far more serious. Jack, meanwhile, had shrunk down in his chair and looked like he wished the ground would swallow him up.

'That's preposterous,' Eric said, waving his hand through the air. 'I made it clear why Erin wasn't originally selected.'

'So, I would be wrong in assuming,' Inés countered, 'that it was Jack who argued most fiercely for Erin not to be selected?'

The senior official raised an eyebrow and looked over at Jack, a question in his eyes, making it clear that Inés' assumption was correct. Jack sat up straighter, regaining his composure. 'My recommendation was that Erin wasn't ready for such a big step up this year. The European stage is a huge one,' he said, addressing the chef d'equipe rather than Inés herself, 'but my reasoning was sound and for the good of the team, which is why the decision was made.'

The chef d'equipe nodded smugly as though satisfied and turned a pitiful gaze on Inés. 'I'm afraid you simply can't go around making accusations of this nature. Whatever personal antagonism lies between you and our selector, I can assure you that Jack is a professional and wouldn't let anything colour his selection process.'

'I see,' Inés answered quietly as she reached into her bag. With the screen open on the threatening message that Jack had sent her, she slid her phone over towards the senior official. 'This is Jack's number, isn't it?' she asked. 'Perhaps you could explain this?'

He looked down at the phone, and when he looked up again his face was white and his eyes cold as they looked at Jack. 'Yes, this does put a different spin on things.' He passed Inés' phone to her and she smiled at Jack, who had gone bright red under the rage-filled glare of the chef d'equipe.

No one moved, so Inés stood up. 'I'll leave you to deal with this. Erin and I are having lunch with the Irish team. I'll be keeping this message and I will let you know if I decide to take any further action.' She turned to leave then stopped and spoke again to Sophie. 'I trust you recorded the team selection meeting? My lawyer may need copies of those files.'

With the final word, Inés bid them good day, offering a nod to Jack and a smile to Eric.

It was difficult to contain her triumph as she exited.

Chapter Twenty

The next morning, Inés and Erin packed their suitcases and prepared to go home. After the events of their trip, they had decided to forgo the few days earmarked for vacation. Inés and Erin wanted to get back to normality. Even the mountain of work she'd have to catch up on seemed appealing. There'd be a pile of stuff waiting for her attention, and she felt so invigorated by how she'd managed to deflate Jack that she wanted to get started sooner rather than later. Inés had been in her position long enough to know she was all but indispensable. She was also missing the rest of her family.

She and Erin had made the most of their last day in Spain. The lunch with the Irish team had gone well, and Inés had a good feeling about Erin's future with them. They seemed down to earth and although Erin was the only girl on the team, Inés suspected that with their focused and fun attitude, Erin would be much more at ease. She'd certainly got along well enough with her new teammates and was excited about her new venture. In fact, Inés hadn't seen her so full of beans for a long time. The team exchanged numbers before Inés and Erin headed off for some retail therapy. *We deserve a treat.*

Inés felt closer to Erin than she ever had. As topsy-turvy and full of drama as their trip had been, it had turned out positive. *Why do you need something bad to experience the good?*

They made their way to Molly's hotel to have a last catch up and a swim in the pool with Tristan before their late evening flight. Inés stretched out on a sunlounger, soaking up the rays before she returned to the English rain, watching Erin and Tristan take turns on the huge water slide at the other end of the pool.

'I wish I'd been there to see Jack's face,' Molly chuckled when Inés finished recounting the tale to her.

'I know. I'd love to know what they said after I left the room. They'll be discreet, of course, but I doubt we'll see Jack next year.'

Molly shook her head. 'No, I think his job's secure there. But what about your threat?'

'It was empty, but they don't know that. I may change my mind as it's now good insurance if they try anything against us in the future, you know?'

They sat in silence for a long moment.

'I'd feel sorry for him if he wasn't such an arse. And of all the women he tried to pull such a trick on, he picked you!' Molly chuckled again.

Inés shrugged. 'Him stalking me is one thing,' she said, pausing to sip her drink, 'but threatening my daughter? No way was I going to stand for that! But I don't think any woman would.'

Molly nodded thoughtfully. 'You know, at breakfast

this morning, one of the other mums – I can't remember her name, Jenny, I think?'

'Jenna,' Inés confirmed.

'Right, her. Well, she's a terrible gossip so I was only half listening, but she said she'd seen Maria and Jack out on their own together last night. Do you think he's moved on to her? She'd eat him for breakfast! And she's married, not that I think she cares.'

'Poor Chelsea,' Inés said.

'You feel sorry for that brat?'

'Well, I don't think she was born like that,' Inés shrugged. She wasn't interested in what Maria or Jack were doing now.

'To be honest,' Molly replied, 'I'm not surprised. They'd make a perfect couple. Albeit temporary. He doesn't have millions in the bank or the social connections Maria is interested in. It's just a fling for her; probably to try and get under your skin.'

'Well, all's well that ends well,' Inés said, in an attempt to change the subject.

'They've got something in common too,' Molly observed. 'Spain hasn't gone particularly well for either of them this year. I do feel sorry for Elizabeth though, and even Ben to a degree. I think they're both easily led.'

'I'll have to pop in and see Elizabeth more,' Inés repeated as if to solidify her promise further. Between the de Bohuns and Charlie and his father, there was plenty going on behind her neighbours' walls.

Inés lay back and tipped her face up to the sun, letting

her thoughts float for a while. She felt like she could drift off into a calming nap. Her reverie was soon interrupted by Molly muttering urgently under her breath. 'Inés, talk of the devil. Look who's turned up. Elizabeth and Maria must be friends again.'

Inés spilled her cocktail as she jumped out of her daydream. She opened her eyes to see Elizabeth and Maria sitting on sunloungers a few feet away. Chelsea was with them, but Ben was absent. She wondered if Elizabeth had finally put her foot down with him and grounded him to his room, but doubted it. Chelsea looked sullen, sitting with her back to her mother, which meant she was facing Inés. Spotting her next to Molly, Chelsea narrowed her eyes and then smirked. Inés ignored her.

Sitting – very close – to Maria was Jack. Inés rolled her eyes behind her sunglasses, wondering how he'd react when he noticed her. She stretched her arms above her head to give the impression she was totally indifferent to his presence.

Elizabeth saw her first and came over with a smile, giving Inés a grateful kiss. 'Thank you so much for the other afternoon, dear,' she gushed. 'I had the most terrible headache and then the shock of Ben being so poorly. I spent the rest of the day in bed.'

Inés smiled, deciding not to contradict Elizabeth's reasoning. 'Don't worry about it. We're friends, right?'

'That's right,' Elizabeth beamed. Then she raised her voice to include Maria and Jack in the conversation. 'How nice we're all together for the final morning! Let's have a drink, shall we?'

Jack looked horrified and Inés wondered how Elizabeth could be so oblivious to everything going on around her.

Erin and Tristan walked over a moment later and Inés saw Erin scowl as her eyes fell on Jack. 'Why is he here?' she said.

'They're with Elizabeth. She's staying at this hotel too,' Molly told her. Erin nodded at Chelsea. 'How are you feeling now?'

'Fine,' Chelsea snapped. She looked over at Inés and a corner of her mouth turned up in a sneer. 'You know mum and Jack are dating now? They make a wonderful couple, don't you think?' She raised her voice so Maria and Jack heard and looked over. Jack looked sheepish, whereas Maria looked at Inés with a haughty look. Inés wondered why on earth they would think she'd care, and exactly what Jack might have told Maria about their ill-fated liaison.

'Yes, they do,' Inés said in a pleasant tone. Chelsea and Maria looked disappointed, while Jack appeared notice-ably relieved. Inés smiled over at them and took a casual sip of her drink, wondering how long it was going to be before Maria made the predictable – and what was becom-ing a boring – jab against her or her family.

'Oh, Inés, I was just talking about you,' Maria trilled.

Less than a minute, Inés thought.

'Oh?' she said pleasantly.

'Yes, I was saying to Jack darling,' Maria said, putting the stress on the darling, 'that I feel terrible for taking such a large price off you for that pony. As I'm sure you've found out by now, he simply won't jump when you want him to. I feel like I didn't take the time to warn you enough, but you were so anxious to have him. I hope you don't think I'm a terribly bad sport.'

'Actually,' Inés said, 'I think he just needed a different rider, because he's coming along tremendously. I spoke to my groom earlier, and he's jumping perfect one-tens at home. He's worth twice what I paid you for him, so I hope you don't think I'm a "terribly bad sport" either.'

Maria's jaw dropped and Inés smiled sweetly before she turned her attention back to the sunshine. She probably should have been angry that Maria had tried to dupe her and was publicly bragging about it, but what was the point? The pony was good. She'd come out of the deal on top, after all.

Erin, however, had no intention of letting go so easily. 'That's nice about your mum and Jack,' she said innocently to Chelsea. 'When did that start?'

'Oh, a few days ago,' Chelsea said airily.

Erin frowned. 'That's odd,' she said, sounding puzzled, 'because he was stalking mum the day before yesterday. I mean, he wouldn't leave her alone, she had to turn her phone off and everything.'

Maria slowly turned to glare at Jack. 'What's she talking about?' she snapped.

Jack immediately looked guilty, and before he could

answer, Maria jumped to her feet and pushed him off his sunlounger before storming off. Looking mortified, Jack started to get to his feet, then slipped on the wet tiles and tumbled straight into the swimming pool with a loud splash. Molly, Erin and Tristan burst out laughing, while Inés, thinking he'd perhaps suffered enough by now, bit her lip to stop her giggles. Still, it seemed the perfect end to their trip.

Chapter Twenty-One

After a day of recuperation from travel, Sunday rolled around and everyone was more than ready for a get-together. Inés wanted to celebrate, since Caoimhe and Erin had done amazingly well. The twins admitted they had a 'fantabulous' time alone with grandma, but Fiadh later told her mother, when she gave them a kiss, 'it was more than enough'.

'Yes, you should pay us for babysitting,' Imogen added. Then Fiadh and Imogen looked at each other, and said simultaneously, 'Granny-sitting!' before scampering off, leaving Inés with a smile. It was good to be home.

Now, she was setting out the tapas her chef had prepared, on the dark marble island in the centre of her kitchen, ignoring Spanky's imploring looks. Tabby sat at the island, a hand on her rapidly growing belly. 'He must be the only dog I know with a taste for Parma ham and scallops. You spoil him, Inés.'

'It's Lily,' Inés said indignantly. 'I caught her feeding him Victoria sponge last month. I'd spent a small fortune on that special diet; now I know why he was getting fat.'

As if she'd heard her name, Lily came skipping into the kitchen. 'When's Uncle Chris coming?' she asked, before trying to climb into Tabby's lap and then thinking better of it. 'You're getting fat,' she announced, before wriggling off again.

'When *is* Chris coming?' Tabby asked. 'Is he bringing this new boyfriend he keeps talking about? Honestly, I've never heard him like this over a guy before.'

'Yes, he just texted. They're on their way. I did suggest my lot might be a bit much for poor Lucas, but he insisted. May as well throw him in the deep end, I suppose.'

'Well, Lily will soon tell him if she doesn't approve.'

The doorbell rang, and Inés heard Jane's voice followed by Chris'. He came into the kitchen looking dapper in jeans and a V-necked jumper, followed by Lucas in trousers so tight they looked as though his circulation was compromised.

Tabby looked as though she was about to fall off her stool. 'Wow,' she mouthed to Inés as she kissed Chris' cheek.

'Uncky Chris!' Lily shouted from behind the adults. She rushed up to him and gave him a huge hug, which he returned before picking her up to introduce Lucas. 'Is he your boyfriend? Are you going to get married?' she chimed. 'He's very handsome but his jeans look uncomfortable.' Lily immediately plopped down on to the floor and made her way to the food, grabbing a sandwich before walking away. She clearly had no time to wait for an answer. Chris smiled after her while Lucas looked confused.

'You have a lovely place,' Lucas said, helping himself

to an olive. Chris smacked Lucas' fingers with a mock offence. 'At least wait till everyone is here,' Chris said.

'Carry on. I'm about to call the rest of the girls in,' Inés told him. 'And thank you. I couldn't imagine living anywhere else now.'

The girls piled on to the food, with Charlie close behind. He had dark shadows under his eyes, Inés noticed, and looked troubled. She longed to know exactly what was going on next door.

Once everyone was seated Inés raised a glass to Erin and Caoimhe, and everyone responded, even Lily and the twins with their fruit juices sporting umbrellas. She'd let Erin, Charlie and Caoimhe have a small glass of Buck's Fizz, and she laughed at Caoimhe's face as she sipped it.

'Uuurgh, I'd rather have a lemonade, mum.'

'Glad to hear it, young lady,' Alice said reprovingly, pretending not to notice Caoimhe's pointed glance at the tall glass of neat whiskey on ice in front of her.

'That's large for lunchtime, mum,' Inés said, shaking her head. She was beginning to wonder if she was the only one who didn't seem to have a drink problem.

'Medicinal,' snapped Alice. 'Good for the constitution.'

After they'd finished eating, the twins and Lily went into the playroom with Jane, while the teenagers dashed off upstairs to watch films. Alice took the bottle to her room, leaving Inés, Tabby, Chris and Lucas to retire to the orangery with a bottle of wine. As soon as they'd got settled, Chris asked the question she knew had been on his lips since he'd arrived.

'Tell all, darling. What happened with Kent the hunk and this Jack person? I couldn't make head nor tail of our phone call. The line from Spain was terrible.'

'What's all this?' Tabby's ears perked up.

Inés told them about Jack, from their disappointing night together to the showdown at the meeting with Eric, and Erin's jibe at Maria's expense.

As she finished, Chris clapped his hands. 'Oh, bravo to you and Erin. That'll make him think twice before he tries something like that again, I'm sure. But what about Kent? You said he came over for lunch?'

Inés wondered why she felt so reluctant to talk about Kent. Now she was home, she felt eager to see him again, but she wasn't sure she wanted to discuss what *could* be. It had occurred to her to invite him today, but she'd decided against it in the end. It was a family occasion, after all, and Inés felt that the lines between them were potentially blurred enough already.

'Yes,' she said breezily. 'He had business nearby, so it made sense to meet up. Jack turned up, actually, and stood there glaring at us. Honestly, he was acting as though I'd cheated on him.'

Tabby shook her head in horror. 'Creep. This is why I'm happier to go it alone,' she said firmly, patting her belly. 'Men are more trouble than they're worth.'

'You mean straight men,' Chris admonished, winking at Lucas, who gave him such a look of adoration that Inés decided maybe they were right for each other after all.

'I still think you should get it on with that teacher,'

Chris said. 'I tell you – I knew he had blue blood. Those cheekbones are to die for.'

'You knew no such thing,' Inés laughed.

'Just think,' Tabby said, 'you'd be a lady.'

'Of precisely nothing,' Inés pointed out. 'He has no inheritance, remember? Besides, he's the girls' teacher. Kent is much more suitable, let's be honest.'

'Damn, Inés. You're not weighing up job options,' Chris teased.

Tabby nodded. 'It's true though. He's rich, handsome … and he already knows the girls. So, when are you seeing him?'

Inés was about to answer that she had no idea, when she heard Jane call from another room: 'The phone's ringing in the hall.' Somehow, she knew it was Kent before she picked it up.

'Friday,' he announced before she could say hello. 'Tell me you're free to come out with me. There's a new French restaurant I want to try, and I need a beautiful woman on my arm.'

'There's lots of those around,' Inés said lightly.

Kent's voice dropped to a deep, Southern drawl that made Inés' lower belly tighten. 'Not for me. Let me rephrase that – I need *you* on my arm.'

'I'll see what I can do,' Inés said casually.

'I'll pick you up at eight,' Kent said, and was gone, leaving Inés staring at the receiver. Kent's ultra-masculine charm was certainly not lost on her; if anything, she found it more attractive than she cared to admit. But she also liked to be in control, and she sensed that Kent was very much the sort of man who wanted to sweep her off her feet. Attempting to keep her feet firmly on the ground, she cradled the receiver and went back into the orangery looking thoughtful.

Chris was on her at once. 'It was Kent, wasn't it? What did he say?'

'He wants to take me for dinner on Friday.'

'Are you going?' asked Lucas.

'Of course she is,' Chris and Tabby said in unison.

'What are you wearing? Not black; the little black dress is so early noughties. How about a nice olive green?' Chris continued.

Inés rolled her eyes and sat down, taking a sip of her drink. 'I'll probably buy something new,' she said.

'Oooh!' Tabby replied, her eyes sparkled. 'Shopping!'

'Who's going shopping?' It was her mother, wandering in to join them, with a plate of muffins. She placed them on the coffee table, giving the muffins a perfect view of the garden.

Tabby promptly took two. 'I'm allowed,' she said through a mouthful of dough, as though daring anyone to challenge her.

'No one,' Inés said quickly, but Chris had already opened his mouth.

'Inés. For her date with Kent on Friday. Although I've told her to wear that new olive green number; the colour is completely on-trend.'

Alice pursed her lips together and shot Inés a

disapproving look. Inés hoped she wasn't going to start going on about George not being at rest again. Sensing the tension, Chris jumped in. 'I bet you had loads of dates when you were a young woman, Alice,' he said, piling on the charm. Her mother had always liked Chris. 'You can certainly see where Inés and the girls get their looks from.'

Alice patted her striking grey hair. 'Thank you, Chris. I did, as a matter of fact. It was quite the scandal in the village where I grew up. I mean, we're talking the sixties in rural Ireland. It wasn't all mini-skirts and the Beatles there. There were two brothers fighting over me, the O'Hara boys, and I was the talk of the town. I didn't like either of them, though my friends did. But every girl needs two men fighting for them at some point in their life. Completely improper, but fun nonetheless.'

'Tell me more,' said Chris, seeming to hang on her every word.

'Yes, do,' Lucas piped up, sounding genuinely interested. 'How did you meet Inés' father?'

Inés suppressed an eye roll as Tabby gave her a sympathetic glance. This story was one she'd heard dozens, if not hundreds, of times before. Still, at least it had stopped her mother lecturing her about Kent and there was something comforting in reminiscing.

'Have a muffin,' Tabby said, currently on her third. 'They really are good.'

But as Inés reached for one, a grey head appeared through the open side door and snatched the remaining two off the plate, making everyone jump.

'Phil!' Inés exclaimed. 'What are you doing?' The pony nickered at her, happily munching on the muffins as a groom ran up behind.

'I'm so sorry, Mrs Cullen.'

'Well, he was due a breakout,' Inés laughed as Phil was led away. 'It's been a while.'

'He was getting a look in on the muffins before Tabby eats them all,' Chris quipped. Tabby swatted him then Alice resumed her story and everyone was now listening intently.

Inés sat back in her chair and grinned as she took another drink. Yes, she was certainly home.

Chapter Twenty-Two

In the end, she did wear black; a simple off-the-shoulder knee-length number, that made the most of her figure while still looking classy. Judging by the look on Kent's face when she got into his car, it was the right choice.

They chatted lightly on the way to the restaurant, and Inés was surprised by how comfortable she felt now she'd finally made the decision to date him and see where it led her. George was gone, and all she could do was trust that her fears around his final moments were false. Somehow, the moment of closure that Erin had come to in Spain had touched Inés, and she felt ready to start a new chapter in her life, even if she didn't know what that was yet.

Kent held her chair out for her and let his fingers brush the top of her bare shoulder as she sat down, and Inés felt a pleasant shiver across her skin. She smiled at him across the table, through the candlelight that flickered between them. It was the opening night of the restaurant, and it was, Inés had to admit, the perfect setting for a romantic first date. Classical music played softly in the background, and the lighting cast a rosy hue over everything. 'This is charming.'

'I'm glad you think so,' Kent said with a smile, looking pleased. 'I hope the food is as good as the place looks.'

Kent was extra attentive, pouring her wine and asking her about herself. Inés chatted about her week at work and the girls, and even told him about her mother's intruder, which made him laugh deeply and slap his broad thigh. When she asked him how his meeting in Spain had gone, however, he seemed suddenly evasive.

'Let's not talk about work,' he said, although he'd just been listening to Inés talk about her first week back at the office. She wondered if he was trying to avoid talking about his previous partnership with George – and herself – and decided that was a wise move. It couldn't have escaped his notice how hesitant she'd been so far, and Kent was astute. She needed to see him as something other than a business acquaintance and friend of George's if this were ever to go anywhere. She raised her glass to him. 'To play, then.'

Kent looked away however, suddenly hesitant. 'What's wrong?' Inés asked. Perhaps he didn't want to talk about work because there was trouble. His next words confirmed her suspicions. 'Nothing, honestly. It's just that work isn't my favourite subject right now. Unusual for me, I know. But I didn't bring you out to talk about that.'

'Don't be silly; you can talk to me. I confided in you about Jack, didn't I? And my fears about George.'

Inés saw a muscle in Kent's jaw twitch as she mentioned the men that had been in her life. Instinctively, she asked: 'Kent? Is this anything to do with George and the business?' She thought again about the odd tax document, the details of which she was still waiting to have confirmed. Did Kent know more than he was telling her?

'In a way …' Kent sighed. 'Inés, I've tried to protect you, because it's what George would have wanted.'

Inés felt an icy hand twist her inside. 'You're not referring to … what I asked … about his death?'

Kent's eyes widened. 'No, Inés, of course not. George felt terrible about letting the business – and you – down, but I'm sure he'd never have willingly left you and the girls. It's nothing as serious as that … just that George left the company in more difficulty than I was prepared to tell you when I bought you out. I've done my best to recoup our losses, but I've never been able to get on top of everything. What with the recent stock market crash … well, we may have to downsize slightly or look for reinvestment. It's a blip, that's all.'

Inés sat back in her chair, and pursed her lips, just as her mother would, in thought. She respected Kent trying to protect her, particularly in the aftermath of George's death, but four years had now passed. She was her own woman, and financially secure. She shook her head. 'You should have come to me before this, Kent. I could have helped.'

Kent smiled wryly. 'I did consider asking you if you wanted to reinvest, but when I saw you and we started getting close – you must know by now I have feelings for you, Inés. I didn't want business matters to interfere with that.' He shook his head in frustration. 'I shouldn't have said anything.'

'You absolutely should have said something, and I wish you had sooner,' she told him. 'And yes, we can certainly look at me reinvesting.'

'Are you sure? I don't want you to be hasty.'

'Well, I'll have to look into the business first. But it's the least I can do as it was George who got you into this mess. We'll set up a meeting. Now,' she grinned at him and raised her glass again, 'can we get back to our date?'

Kent smiled, the relief on his face apparent. This time he joined her in her toast. 'To us,' he announced, 'in business and pleasure.'

When the first course came, the food was as divine as the place looked, and Inés felt herself letting go and enjoying the moment, any lingering doubts evaporating. She was glad he'd finally confided in her; it lifted any remaining tension. She was intrigued by the idea of a partnership – in more ways than one. Kent had a commanding presence; it was hard not to get swept away by his charisma, and Inés had had enough of trying. When he took her hand over the table, she squeezed his boldly, and when his thigh brushed hers underneath it, she responded by slipping her foot out of her stiletto and rubbing his ankle. Kent's eyes were dark with desire as he held her gaze.

'Shall we have dessert back at mine?' he asked, and for the first time she saw a flicker of anxiety in his eyes, as though he expected her to decline.

Inés took a sip of her drink thoughtfully, then met his eyes over the glass and smiled slowly. 'Yes,' she said, her voice a purr. 'Let's do that.'

Back at Kent's house, they were barely through the door before they were in each other's arms, kissing each other with a hunger that Inés felt all the way down to her toes. She abandoned any thought of the tensions of the past few weeks as his mouth explored hers gently and his hands buried themselves in her hair; she let herself melt into him. Her skin burned with lust as pent-up desire rushed to the surface without guilt to hold it back. She couldn't help but allow a sultry smile to play across her face.

Kent slowly unzipped her dress and she stepped out of it, letting it fall to the floor.

Though dressed only in stilettos and underwear while Kent was fully clothed, Inés felt powerful in his company, in this situation, adding to her arousal. He took her hand and led her up the stairs of his Chelsea mews house. And at the doorway to his bedroom he hesitated, his hand resting lightly on her hip, and he kissed her again cautiously, his lips lingering on hers.

'I've always wanted you, Inés,' he breathed into her ear. Inés kissed him again and he groaned low in his throat. His eagerness showed when he all but pulled her into his bedroom. She tugged at his jacket, before unbuttoning his shirt. Kent wasn't going to wait and neither was she. He took a step back and stripped it off, revealing a honed, broad physique with a smattering of neat, salt and pepper coloured hair across his chest that tapered into a thin line and disappeared below his belt. Inés traced it with her fingers, looking up at him with a wicked smile dancing around the corners of her lips.

Kent ran his large hands slowly over the contours of her body, so delicately that his touch created a swelling deep in her abdomen. He traced her curves with his thick palms and lingered over her breasts and hips as she stood there exposed to his yearning. His eyes – dark with desire – roamed, clearly enamoured with what he saw. Holding his gaze, Inés reached around and unclasped her bra, allowing her breasts to fall into his hands. He slid her bra down her arms and palmed her breasts delicately. Her nipples stiffened against the touch of his skin and she felt delicious jolts flood through her body to her groin, intensifying as he pushed her breasts together and bent his head to gently kiss her nipples. She gasped as he drew one slowly into his mouth, glancing up at her as he did so.

Then he knelt down in front of her and kissed the delicate skin in the dip of her hip bones as he slid her panties down her thighs. Inés stepped out of them and reached for Kent's belt.

Within moments, they were naked and Kent was laying her back on the bed almost reverently, sliding her stilettos off her feet. Then he knelt above her and looked down at her with something like triumph in his eyes. 'I've fantasised about this so many times,' he said, 'and now here you are. I intend to take my time.'

He kissed and nibbled at her neck while his hand travelled lightly up the inside of her thighs, exploring her body. Inés opened to him, moaning lightly when he kissed his way, maddeningly slowly, all the way down the front of her body and then back up her thighs before finally reaching his destination. Inés sighed. Kent knew exactly what he was doing, and he teased and tasted her with part finesse, part raw passion. His groans of pleasure prompted her further towards orgasm. Inés gasped as she felt it building, opening her legs wider and arching her back as she climaxed, her fingers bunched in his hair.

She shuddered; her smile languid in the afterglow of her pleasure. Kent raised himself on his arms above her, a raw need in his face that made her feel wanted, desired, craved. He went to position himself in between her legs, but Inés shook her head with a smile.

'My turn,' she said. She pushed lightly at his chest and Kent did as she gestured, lying on his back and looking at her. For a second there was something oddly vulnerable in his eyes, replaced by lust when Inés took him in her hands and then her mouth.

She took her time, bringing him to the brink and back again, enjoying how he was putty in her hands, his hands bunching into fists as he gripped the sheets, gasping her name through gritted teeth as he tried to retain some control. When she'd teased him enough, Inés sat astride him and moved, slowly and rhythmically, bringing herself to another orgasm on top of him.

'My turn,' Kent repeated. He rolled her on to her back and reared above her, holding her gaze while he thrust deeply inside her. Inés gripped his shoulders. She'd missed this feeling of a man between her thighs, inside her, desiring her. A thrill went through her as he groaned and thrust deep. He called her name as he held her in a tight embrace, and they lay panting for a moment.

Afterwards she lay on his chest, her limbs heavy, and yawned with contentment as Kent lazily stroked her hair. She could stay here, satisfied, forever.

'Stay,' he said, curling a lock of her hair around his fingers.

'I will have to leave early, before the kids are up and roaming around,' she pointed out, 'but yes.'

'I'll wake you up and make sure you're off in time,' he told her, his voice becoming heavy with sleep. Inés' own eyelids were fluttering.

Just as she was dropping off, she could have sworn that Kent had murmured 'I love you,' into her hair, but before she could process his words, she'd fallen asleep and they were forgotten.

• • •

Inés woke up to the rising sun streaming through the blinds and the smell of fresh coffee. She sat up, smiling as she remembered the night before. 'What's the time?'

'Half past five,' Kent said, his eyes creased from sleep. Inés groaned. 'Well, you said you needed to get up early.'

'I did, and I do. But,' Inés wriggled sensuously under the sheet, 'it's so comfortable, I could stay here all day.'

Kent sat down next to her, trailing his fingers across her naked collarbone. 'I can't think of anything better than having you in my bed all day. I appreciate you need to be there for the girls. It's one of the things I love about you; you're an amazing mother.'

Love.

Inés felt flattered and unsettled by the prospect of growing this relationship further. When Kent leaned forward and kissed her softly, igniting a flare of desire low in the pit of her belly, she decided to think about it later.

She kissed him back, harder, and heard him growl softly low in his throat before he pulled away. 'Stop,' he protested, 'or I'll be tempted to make you stay.'

Inés laughed lightly as she reached for the bagel and coffee he'd graciously brought up while she was still sleeping. Kent slid into bed next to her. 'What are your plans for this morning?' she asked.

'I'm going back to sleep once you've gone,' he laughed, 'but I'll be up again at eight for a run. Then I have a meeting online. No rest for the wicked, I'm afraid.'

Chapter Twenty-Three

Inés was drinking coffee, while signing Lily's reading book. A normal weekday morning in the Cullen household. Swallowing her avocado, she put Lily's book into her school bag and looked at Alice, who was standing in the doorway with her hands on her skinny hips.

'I had no sleep last night, there was scratching around in the attic; footsteps through the house; doors banging. All night!' Alice complained for the third time. 'It's no good at my age; I need my rest.'

'I know, Mum,' Inés said soothingly. 'But no one else has heard or seen the intruder you keep talking about. And we have an alarm, and I'm sure Spanky would bark.'

'So, let's ignore the mad old lady, shall we?' Alice snapped, glaring at her daughter. Inés closed her eyes and counted slowly to five, determined to remain patient.

'Mum, that's not the case at all,' she said softly. 'Of course I take it seriously. I'm going to phone the security firm today and see about getting cameras installed, okay? We have them for the yard.'

'Well, that's a start,' Alice huffed. 'But, what if the intruder can't be picked up on camera? I'm telling you, something is trying to get our attention.'

'Maybe we have bats. I'll get pest control out.'

Alice tutted. 'I know what bats sound like, young lady. This intruder isn't from this side of the veil at all.'

'Not in front of Lily,' Inés warned.

'It's okay, I know granny believes in ghosts,' Lily said seriously, making it clear she thought her grandmother's views were the height of silliness. 'But I think it's fairies.'

Inés suppressed a smile. 'Come on, cheeky monkey, it's time for school. Remember, it's parent's evening tonight.'

Lily looked excited. 'Mr Taylor is doing a talk, mum!' she said.

'He seems like a nice young man,' Alice said, looking pointedly at Inés then to Lily, who'd probably been spinning granny tales of how Raff was in love with mummy and they should get married. She was already aware of what her mother thought of Kent. He was too flash and too *American* for her tastes.

'You sound like Chris,' she sighed. Then she got up and ushered Lily out of the kitchen before Alice could respond. 'Twins!' she yelled up the stairs. 'Hurry up if you want a lift.'

Fiadh and Imogen came clattering down the stairs, looking like such mirror images of each other that it even took Inés a few moments to tell them apart. Erin and Caoimhe had already left. Inés packed the kids into the car and drove to the school, thinking about her mother's comment. She hadn't set eyes on Raff since coming back from Spain, which was now nearly two weeks ago, and she hadn't thought about him. Now he'd been mentioned, however, his handsome face came sharply to mind. She dropped off the children at the school gate and craned her head out of the car window to see if he was in the playground, feeling disappointed when he wasn't.

Back at the house, a delivery man stood on her doorstep with a huge bouquet of flowers in his hands. She smiled as she took them from him. The bouquet was so huge that she had to turn sideways to get through the double front doors without damaging the petals. As she walked into the kitchen, Alice looked up with a scowl. 'Again? That's the second one this week. They'll play havoc with my allergies.'

'They can go in the orangery. And you don't have any allergies.'

Alice sniffed haughtily. 'It's suspicious, if you ask me. Men only buy flowers when they're guilty about something.'

'Nonsense,' Inés said briskly. 'George used to bring me flowers all the time.'

Alice's face softened. 'Ah, yes. But George was a special man, God rest his soul.'

Inés wondered what her mother would say if she knew her sainted son-in-law had left his business partner in such a mess. But she'd never reveal this to her mother. There was nothing to be gained in upsetting her. *Let the memories of the dead lie untroubled.*

'He was,' she said softly as she found a vase and started arranging the flowers in it. Calling her florist, Esther, Inés hoped that she could hide behind a voicemail. Inés had been using Esther for years. They had built a good relationship over time as Esther knew how important a well-presented home was to Inés.

'Hello, Esther,' Inés said pleasantly when she answered the phone, hoping she wouldn't cause too much hassle. 'I'm afraid I need to cancel next week. I'll still pay your retainer of course, considering the short notice.'

Esther said awkwardly: 'Inés, this is the third time this month. If you're using someone else now, I'd appreciate it if you'd let me know.'

'It isn't that,' Inés hastened. 'I've just had a lot of flowers sent to me recently.'

'Oh? A new admirer, then?' Esther asked, sounding eager for gossip.

Inés brushed over the comment. 'Like I said, things will be back to normal next week, so I'll see you as usual. I'll still pay you for the three visits you've missed lately.'

As she replaced the phone, Inés decided she'd have to ask Kent to stop sending flowers, lovely as they were. Esther had been with her a long time, and she could appreciate that her florist was worried about losing a regular and well-paying client. But aside from anything else, Esther knew Inés' taste better than Kent.

As she turned around, she saw Alice in the doorway to the lounge, watching her suspiciously. Inés sighed. Sometimes, her mother treated her as though she was no older than Erin.

Alice narrowed her eyes. 'So, when are you seeing this Kent person again?'

'Mum,' Inés protested, 'this "Kent person" has been

a family friend for twenty years now. It's not as though you've never met him. But to answer your question, I'm seeing him on Friday.'

As Alice opened her mouth to respond, there was a knock on the door. Relieved, Inés went to open it, although she hoped for Esther's sake that it wasn't a second bouquet. A courier stood there with a letter in his hand. She took it, wondering what was so important that it needed a signature.

Inés went to the lounge to open it, noticing the stamp on the front with foreboding. She pulled out the letter and unfolded it, reading it with a frown. Then she pressed the back of her hand to her mouth.

The government wanted to look over George and Kent's company finances. The same company Kent now wanted her to reinvest in. She laid the letter down on the coffee table, her thoughts racing. This wasn't just about a mistake, or outstanding tax. This meant a suspicion of serious fraud.

Inés felt sick. She knew George had got into a financial mess. Reckless spending, unpaid debts – but fraud? That was something else entirely. And if this came out, William would definitely call her professional integrity into question. Her job could be at risk, not to mention her home, if she was found liable. She had to speak to Kent. She reached for her phone, flicked through to his number, and then paused as a new thought occurred to her.

Did he know? Was that why he'd been so reluctant to tell her how much trouble George had left the company in? She wasn't a child that needed protecting.

Inés stared out of the windows of the orangery, her mind swarming with worries, her body motionless with indecision.

Chapter Twenty-Four

Inés walked into the school hall holding Lily's hand, looking around for her class teacher. She spotted Miss Hawker behind a desk piled high with schoolbooks and walked over to take a seat, Lily skipping alongside her. Miss Hawker smiled indulgently at Lily as they sat down.

'There isn't much I can say about Lily,' Miss Hawker said, 'other than to tell you how pleased I am with her. She's an absolute delight to teach, and such an individual character.'

Inés grinned, thinking that was the biggest understatement she'd heard for a while. 'And her schoolwork?'

'Ahead of all her targets,' Miss Hawker said proudly.

Lily wriggled in her seat. 'Can we go now?'

Miss Hawker passed over Lily's schoolbooks for Inés to look through, filled with brightly coloured pictures and her daughter's early attempts at writing. No matter how many times Inés had done this with her children, she still loved it. She felt a twinge of sadness at the thought that Lily was growing up fast, and there would soon be no more early years parent's evenings.

After their allocated ten minutes were up, Inés took Lily's hand and walked around the hall, looking politely at the various children's projects that had been showcased and the class information boards. She heard footsteps behind her and turned to see Raff.

'Hello,' Lily chirped.

'Hello, Lily, Inés. How are you?' His serious hazel eyes settled on hers, and Inés had a sudden urge to confide in him. She felt he'd be a good listener.

'I'm great, thank you,' she said instead. 'And you?'

'I'm pretty well. How was Spain?'

'Erin is Irish now,' Lily said seriously, and Inés laughed, which disrupted the sudden awkwardness. She told Raff about Spain and Erin's win – leaving out the sorry tale of Jack – and felt disappointed when she realised the event was coming to an end. Lily's appointment had been one of the last.

'I should go,' she said apologetically. 'You need to pack away.'

'I'll walk you out,' said Raff.

A few of the other parents looked at them with curiosity as they made their way out of the hall. Raff walked her out to the car park, then hung around as she strapped Lily into the back seat and swung her door shut.

'Is everything okay?'

'Erm, yes, I just,' Raff began awkwardly, then the rest of his words came out in such a rush that he tripped over them, 'was wondering if you wanted to go grab a drink or something this Friday?'

Shocked, Inés hesitated. 'Oh, um. Well,' she said carefully, 'well, you see, the thing is…' She gave him an imploring look, searching for help in his face. She didn't want to mention her date with Kent, although there was no reason why she shouldn't. Nor was there a good reason why she was feeling flustered. A simple no would do, instead, 'I'm afraid I have a date on Friday,' popped out. She looked for something to kill the awkward silence. He looked so pained. Feeling like she'd kicked a puppy and wanting to make the situation better, she continued, 'but thank you for the offer'.

Raff looked as though he wanted a car to plough him down. 'Oh, of course. Well, sorry to have kept you. Um. I'll see you at the school, no doubt. Good day.' He turned and quickly walked away, leaving Inés staring after him as she processed what had happened.

Lily fell asleep on the back seat and Inés thought about the events of the day. After she'd read and re-read the letter ten times, she'd decided not to call Kent. He'd already told her that he'd be incredibly busy this week, and this wasn't something that could be discussed in a quick phone call – she needed to talk to him in person. She'd speak to him Friday. In the meantime, she had to set up a meeting with her accountant, something she should've done weeks ago, to go over the old figures and see what she could spot. None of this made any sense. She didn't want to believe that George could possibly have been capable of this – but the evidence seemed to be staring her in the face.

After putting Lily to bed and ensuring everyone else was settled, Inés went up to the attic where there were still boxes of George's old papers she'd never fully looked at. Now, she wondered if they might be able to tell her anything. Below her, one by one, she heard each family member making their way to bed. The house grew quieter and Inés searched on, watched by a small brown mouse hiding under some rolls of old wallpaper. She found a few papers relating to the company, but nothing was in order and there was seemingly a great deal missing. After endless read-throughs and attempts to tally up the figures, there were too many gaps in her knowledge of the business. She continued well into the small hours, determined. The mouse finally grew bored and left.

She looked at the bottom line, denominated everything to its basic form. The balance sheet never lied. The company had made huge gains and huge losses, but Inés couldn't work out why and where this money had gone. On top of this, it seemed at different points in time, the company had more money than it should have. Some of the outgoings made sense on paper, but her gut told her this didn't translate to how the books should look. She collected everything she could find, but the intent to pass them on to her accountant first was waning. She trusted her accountant, but something was wrong. After a long thoughtful moment, she phoned Chris.

Though Chris had one of the most skilled minds with figures that she knew, they'd agreed not to mix their friendship with work, so Inés had never asked him to get involved in her finances before. *But this was different.*

Chris whistled through his teeth when she explained the situation. 'This sounds serious, Inés, as well as – I mean, George? Really?' his voice sounded groggy, she'd probably woken him up.

'My thoughts exactly,' Inés said. 'It makes no sense. Do you think he was funding something, or lent money out of the business and didn't get to pay it back?'

'It's possible, but again, George? Look Inés, scan them over and I'll see if I can make any sense of it. It might take a few days before I can get to it, but I'll do my best.'

'Thank you,' Inés said gratefully, although as she put the phone down she felt a sense of foreboding. She had a horrible feeling that she was going to dredge up things she'd wish she'd never found out. *Some ghosts should remain undisturbed.* Yet, she couldn't shake her fear. Perhaps George had been trying to tell her something, after all?

Chapter Twenty-Five

By the time Friday came around, Inés had steeled herself to confront Kent. He must have known more than he was letting on, and Inés was starting to wonder how much she could trust him. Her patience was fast becoming tested. Even if his motives were honourable, letting her reinvest in the company without being upfront about the possible embezzlement was unforgivable. She reminded herself of her work mantra: *don't trust anyone.* The more she thought about it, the clearer her thoughts became. Inés also felt certain that if George had done this, there was no way he'd done it alone – Kent had to have been part of it. And Inés wasn't going to take this lying down. Rather than confront Kent in anger, however, she decided to play this carefully. Getting Kent to tell her the full story needed more finesse. She got dressed for their date, her choice of clothes more risqué than usual. It didn't hurt to use all the tools you had at your disposal.

She waited for the cab to take her to the theatre where they were meeting, making sure she looked a million dollars. Her hair was freshly cut and dried and she wore a cream cashmere dress that hugged her body like a second skin. When she stepped out of the cab, Kent looked at her with admiration.

'Darling,' he said, kissing her cheek, 'you look stunning.'

'Thank you,' Inés murmured demurely. He looked incredibly handsome himself in chinos and a blazer. She felt the pull of his allure as she caught a scent of his after-shave. Her thoughts drifted to their night together. It had been a long time since she'd had that kind of experience, and as much as she wanted it again, she needed to keep her head. As much as she wanted to give him the benefit of the doubt and hope he knew nothing about the possible fraud, tax evasion, embezzlement – whatever it was – she was suspicious enough to put the brakes on any feelings she might have had developing for him. The idea that Kent might be taking her for a fool was more than she could bear. Even so, she smiled sweetly and took Kent's arm as he led her into the theatre.

They were watching a new play that had received rave reviews, but Inés was too distracted to fully get into the story – it was something unnecessarily complex about the Edwardian era, punctuated by long boring monologues.

Kent didn't look too impressed, either. Halfway through he put his hand on her thigh and leaned over to whisper in her ear: 'This is pretty dull, isn't it? Why don't we get outta here?'

His meaning was unmistakable. For a moment Inés was tempted, remembering how exciting the sex had been – she wanted that again; to be satisfied. But more than that, she wanted to be wanted. She wanted so desperately to share intimate moments with someone. Mostly, she wanted a partner, to share the burdens and pleasures of life. The temptation was overwhelming. *Perhaps she could throw caution to the wind and deal with the fall out later?*

She shook her head primly. She couldn't allow herself. 'I'm enjoying it,' she said, not meeting Kent's eyes but keeping them fixed on the stage. Kent leaned back in his seat.

After the play had finished, they went up to the theatre's VIP bar for cocktails. Inés couldn't keep up the act any longer. She had to know. Before she could say anything, however, Kent brought up the subject himself.

'So, I've been talking to my finance manager about setting up a meeting this week to explore our options for you reinvesting,' he began. His words were tentative. 'I must say, it's going to be amazing to have you back on board.'

His eyes twinkled and, for a moment, Inés' suspicions faltered. This was Kent, for goodness' sake. He wouldn't do anything to hurt her or the girls, surely? But then, she reminded herself, she'd said the same about George, yet there had clearly been something going on. 'Actually,' Inés said carefully, 'there's a few things I need to discuss with you. I'm afraid I may not be able to reinvest after all.'

'Why?' Kent's tone was light, but there was a sudden flash of rage in his eyes – a rage that she'd seen before – so intense that it startled her. It left his face as swiftly as it had appeared.

Inés took the letter from her bag, smoothed it out and laid it on the table in front of him. She studied Kent's face carefully as he read and saw the muscles twitch around his left eye. 'I don't understand,' he said. 'What's this about?' He looked and sounded utterly convincing, but Inés didn't believe him; her instincts were screaming at her that something was badly wrong. Was the excitement she felt for Kent really anxiety?

'Exactly what it says. Your company, back when it belonged to you and George – and me, as a shareholder – is being investigated for fraud. You must have had one of these yourself, Kent. It's time you started being honest with me.' She held back on the accusations she wanted to hurl at him. But she'd been through this conversation in her head a hundred times, she knew every possible outcome and had an answer for each of them. She'd play this out without any loss of emotional or intellectual control, in order to get to the bottom of things.

Kent pulled a hand down his stubbled cheek, not meeting her eyes. He stared into the distance thoughtfully, as though pondering how much to tell her.

'I need to know the truth, Kent,' Inés insisted. 'It's going to come out now, anyway. We have no kind of future – professionally or in any other way – if you lie to me now.'

Kent nodded. 'Of course. But please understand, Inés,' he met her eyes, looking completely sincere, 'I was only ever trying to protect you.'

'By asking me to invest money into a business that's being investigated for fraud?'

'I had no idea this was going to happen. Yes, I got the same letter, but it was as much of a shock to me as it was to you. I asked you to reinvest in good faith, because the company can be saved. I honestly thought this was in the past.'

Inés took a deep breath. 'So, you did know?'

Kent looked down, his face full of remorse. 'Yes. Not until after George had died, of course, and then it became apparent that it wasn't just debt that was the problem – he'd been embezzling funds in an attempt to recoup his losses without anyone finding out.'

'But you didn't report it?' Her question pushed him further into a corner.

Kent looked pained. 'Inés, how could I? Not only would my reputation be affected, but what would that have done to you, a grieving widow with five children, one a tiny baby? It hadn't come out, and so I decided the best thing to do was to hush it up as much as I could and try and get the business back on its feet. Until recently, I thought it was going that way. Now this – this could ruin us.'

'I knew nothing about it,' Inés snapped. 'You covered it up. And you expect me to believe you knew nothing? You're not that naïve, Kent. George couldn't have done this on his own. He was a good man, and honest to a fault.'

Again there was a flash of anger, and Inés began to wonder how well she knew Kent.

'He wasn't that honest, Inés,' Kent pointed out, sounding offended now, 'because he didn't tell you how much trouble he was in, did he? But I can assure you, I knew nothing about this until after his death. I was as shocked as you. Yes, I should have told you, but can you blame me for trying to protect you? I've loved you for years, Inés, and I felt guilty about it when you were married to George. The least I could do for you after his death was to keep you from finding out about this.'

He seemed sincere, and Inés heard a ring of truth when he confessed his feelings for her. His explanation made perfect sense, but for one thing: Kent could have come to her about this, one, or even two years after George had passed away. But he didn't. He was admitting this now because *she* had found out. She knew something. She backed him into a corner and gave him no choice but to come clean.

Inés put her hand to her forehead, feeling the beginnings of a headache, as well as confusion. She didn't know what to think. 'I have my accountant looking through George's files, what I have of them,' she said eventually. 'You must have more records, I imagine?' For some reason, she'd decided not to tell him she'd asked Chris to look through them as well.

He glanced at her sharply, but when he spoke his voice was smooth. 'There's no need,' he said. 'Bring me George's files and I'll get our guy to go through everything. He knows the business inside out and will have better context. Together we can see where we're at.'

'Hmm,' Inés said, non-committal. She drained her glass and put it down. 'I think I'm going to call it a night,' she said. 'This is an awful lot to take in and I've had a busy week at the office. I need to rest.'

'Of course,' Kent said, gentlemanly again. 'I'll get a cab with you.'

'Isn't it out of your way?'

'I want to make sure you get home safely.'

Inés decided not to argue, and they went outside together and hailed a cab. Kent looked sad, and Inés wondered if she'd misjudged him. *Perhaps he hadn't known.* Her judgement faltered. Was she being overly suspicious? But she needed that to be confirmed before she could continue whatever was happening between them.

'I hope this isn't going to affect us, Inés,' Kent said softly as the cab drove down the long country roads towards the yard.

'I hope so too,' Inés said, distant but sincere, and when Kent's fingers brushed hers on the seat, she had to find the determination to snatch them away.

When the cab pulled up outside, Inés paid for her part of the fare and got out. As she turned to say goodbye to Kent, she stared in surprise as he got out too and the car started to pull off.

'Let me come in for a coffee,' he said.

She frowned at him, annoyed. 'The girls are in bed.'

'I know. I do mean just coffee. I don't want to leave things the way they are tonight … for this to come between us. I've only ever tried to do my best, Inés.'

He looked so forlorn that against her better judgement, Inés nodded. 'Okay. One coffee.'

As she opened the door, he stood uncomfortably close behind her, so she stepped away quickly into the hall.

'Take a seat in the lounge,' she said, hanging up her coat. Kent made for the room at the end of the hallway.

The green light of her answering machine blinked insistently and she pressed it without thinking.

It was Chris.

'Inés, call me in the morning,' he said, sounding serious. 'It's hard to say for certain but there are definitely discrepancies in George's papers. What's weird is the underlined bits – it's as though George was investigating himself. I could be wrong, but I don't think this is as straightforward as we first thought. Just … call me.' It beeped off, leaving Inés staring at it. She wondered if Kent had heard.

'Do you take sugar?' she called out.

'Two, darling,' he answered, and Inés breathed a sigh of relief.

She went into the kitchen and looked in bemusement at the open door that led to the utility room. Inés was certain it had been shut when she went out. *Surely Jane wouldn't be doing laundry at midnight.* She checked the back door, realising with a shudder that it was unlocked. *I know I locked up before I went out.* She thought about Alice's mysterious intruder and wondered if she were starting to get paranoid. Shaking her head, she made the coffees and carried them through to the lounge. Kent's eyes didn't leave her as she placed the cups on the coffee table and sat down.

'Who was that on the machine?' he asked, an edge to his voice.

He'd heard.

'Chris,' she answered, matter-of-factly. 'I asked him to have a look through some papers for me.'

'*My* papers?'

'*George's* papers.'

'I said there was no need.'

Reality burst around Inés' ears with an almighty clatter. And she understood what she'd been denying for weeks. 'It was you, wasn't it? Not George. It was you all along.'

Kent's face was expressionless. Inés shook her head, feeling frozen with anger. 'How could you?' she said through gritted teeth. 'He trusted you. You were his best friend. And you used his death for your convenience, to put the blame on him!'

Kent didn't reply.

Inés felt sick. 'You must have been glad he died,' she accused.

Kent sneered at her, his face twisted with a menace she'd never seen in him before. 'Oh, my darling Inés,' he said, 'you don't get it, do you?'

'Don't get what?' she asked, bewildered.

Kent gave a bitter laugh. The glee on his face betraying what he'd done. And it was so obvious Inés wondered how this hadn't occurred to her before. 'You killed him,' she said flatly.

A heavy silence stung the air as Inés waited for Kent to deny it, to act offended or shocked, or insist she was wrong. She badly wanted to be wrong. *Please let me be wrong, then this can be over.*

Instead, Kent gave her a slow handclap, his face twisted into an ugly taunt that made him almost unrecognisable. Inés felt an icy hand grip her heart. She was looking at her husband's murderer. All Inés could think about was her family, sleeping soundly, just feet away.

'Well done,' Kent said in a perfectly calm voice that was all the more chilling for its lack of emotion. 'Yes, I did. George was starting to poke around and it wouldn't be long before he discovered what was happening. I didn't plan it, but then I saw him, standing on the edge of the yacht, drunk, and it seemed so simple. So … easy. Like the moment had been set up, just for me, by some divine entity. So, I pushed him overboard. No one suspected a thing.'

Inés fought the sensation of vomit climbing up her throat. 'You *monster*,' she hissed, shaking with shock and rage, her sense of vulnerability forgotten for a moment.

Kent shrugged. 'He deserved it,' he said coldly. 'George didn't appreciate what he had … especially with you. He didn't deserve you. He told me the two of you were considering an open marriage. What kind of fool allows that? He wasn't man enough to keep you happy. He didn't deserve you, or the girls, or the business.'

'You were jealous of him,' Inés realised. 'All that time, you wanted everything he had. Enough to kill him for it, and he loved you like a brother.'

Inés remembered his hands on her body and was repulsed. Anxiety began to swell in her stomach. She'd thought his feelings for her were real. They felt real. *How could she have got this so wrong?*

'He was a fool,' Kent snapped.

Inés jumped to her feet. 'Get out,' she ordered, her legs trembling. 'I want you out of my house.'

Kent rose slowly to his feet, but instead of leaving he took a step closer to Inés. She was cornered; she tensed, her skin prickling and her breath catching in her throat.

'I can't,' he said softly. 'Not now.'

It was at that point Inés understood how much danger she was in. She went to bolt past him, darting to the side, but although she was nimble, Kent was too big for her to get past him easily. He swung an arm around her middle and forced her back down on to the couch as she fought him, bucking against his hold with all her might. Unable to get her arms free she kicked him, but although he winced with pain, he knelt on her legs, preventing her from trying the same trick again. Inés opened her mouth to scream, with rage as much as with fear.

'Make a sound,' Kent warned her, 'and I'll be forced to silence the girls, too.'

She froze in terror at his words and she thought about the girls and her mother upstairs, sleeping peacefully. She heard a thump against the kitchen door and a low growling. Spanky could sense she was in danger. If only she hadn't shut the door. She tried to think, to make some kind of plan, but suddenly Kent's hands were around her throat and she couldn't make a sound.

'You shouldn't have told Chris,' Kent said, his voice sing-song as he began choking the life out of her. She felt her chest tighten and constrict, but she fought not to lose consciousness, determined not to give up so easily. Inés clawed at his face, peeling off her nail in the process. Her fingers found his eye socket, and she pushed in, causing him to yelp and loosen his grip. He growled in a rage that frightened her even more. She whipped round and tried to scramble over the back of the sofa, but Kent grabbed her dress before she could vault over it and pulled her down roughly, kneeling on her again and pushing her face into the cushion. With his weight pressing down on her painfully, she was now well and truly trapped.

'Shhh,' Kent whispered above her, like a lover would whisper into the ear of their partner.

Inés struggled with all her might despite feeling her efforts were futile. She'd fight to the death if she had to – it was starting to look as though that was exactly what she was doing. Kent' s hands were around her neck, squeezing again, and she was growing weaker as she gasped for a breath she couldn't take. Dark spots danced in front of her eyes, and her chest felt as though it was about to explode. She tried to fight against the blackness, thinking of the girls upstairs in their beds. They couldn't come down and find her like this.

Her mind began to drift and she wondered if her murder would be blamed on Alice's otherwise invisible intruder; the mysterious ghost providing the perfect scapegoat for Kent's evil. Inés mustered the last of her strength and threw herself back desperately, wrenching her neck back in the hope of connecting the back of her head with his face. Kent was too strong. Although she managed to connect with bone and elicit a grunt of pain, he forced her back down and tightened his grip as she felt her consciousness ebbing away. Her throat burning with a pain that drove her quieter, quieter, until blackness was all she knew.

Chapter Twenty-Six

A great weight fell away and her mouth involuntarily opened as air rushed into her lungs. Taking a breath had never felt so sweet. Relief washed over her whole body as her throat caught at the dragging breath entering her lungs. Kent rolled away from her and she heard him hit the ground with a thud. Breathing in huge gulps, she sat up to see a familiar figure towering over her, holding the marble rolling pin from the kitchen.

'What are you doing here?' It was a flesh and blood figure that stood in front of her, and certainly no ghost.

'Surprise,' he offered meekly with a worried smile. 'I'm your mysterious intruder,' he said apologetically.

Thank God. Charlie.

At the sight of Charlie, rolling pin raised, looking down at Kent's inert form lying on the floor, Inés had wondered briefly if she were hallucinating; if Kent's hands around her throat had caused her black out and dream, or worse, was she dead? The situation was too surreal to make any sense, and Inés had experienced a strong urge to giggle, a reaction she later attributed to shock. Instead, she righted herself, swinging her feet to the floor and stared up at Charlie, still wondering if he was real.

Charlie, too, had looked to be in shock, his dark eyes huge in his pale face as he stared down at Kent. 'Have I … killed him?'

Inés knelt down and saw Kent's chest rising and falling, and in that moment couldn't have said if she was relieved or disappointed. 'I think we need to call the police,' she'd said in a faraway voice.

'And maybe an ambulance?' Charlie suggested, still staring at Kent and fiddling with the rolling pin in his hands.

Inés nodded. 'That, too, I suppose.'

At that moment, Erin and Caoimhe piled into the lounge, looking faintly guilty as they looked at Charlie. Then they spotted the rolling pin and Kent on the floor. Erin had looked as though she'd faint, while Caoimhe simply asked: 'What's going on, mum?'

'Come here, girls.' Inés rose and pulled her precious daughters into a mamma-bear hug, never wanting to let them go.

'He tried to kill me,' Inés answered in a matter-of-fact tone. *And he killed your father* she thought, reality finally breaking through. Tears filled her eyes as Erin pulled her in even tighter.

Charlie phoned the emergency services, and then they stood in a ragged circle around Kent's unconscious form, no one daring to speak or take their eyes off of him. Inés leaned on Erin, grateful for her eldest daughter's strength.

It was only later, after Kent came round in the back of

the ambulance – threatening Inés' life again, with shouts from the bed he was now handcuffed to – that Inés and Charlie had time to talk. Inés asked Charlie why he'd been in her house, and why no one but her had been particularly surprised by his presence.

It had turned out that Caoimhe and Erin had been disabling the house alarm and letting Charlie in for months whenever his father came home drunk and raging. Charlie was liable to bear the brunt of his father's wrath, and so he'd been sneaking into their house, sleeping in Caoimhe's room and then sneaking out again in the early hours. The twins had eventually been in on it too, letting Charlie in while the rest of them were in Spain. Spanky hadn't been barking at the intruder because, of course, Spanky didn't see Charlie as an intruder.

Alice was right after all. 'See!' she'd said loudly, often and to anyone who would listen. 'I told you I wasn't crazy when I was hearing things!'

'Yes, mother, we will never doubt you again,' Inés had said faintly. 'And I'm relieved. At least there wasn't a ghost.'

• • •

It was the last Friday of the month, Jane's day off and Inés' half-day at work. As she loaded the dishwasher, glancing at the clock to see that Lily and the twins would need picking up in twenty minutes, her thoughts drifted to the past week. It hadn't been easy, that was for certain. In fact, it had been such a rollercoaster of emotion that Inés wasn't sure when, if ever, things would get back to normal. She supposed there'd be a new normal from now on.

Once the shock had worn off and Inés had started to feel more like herself, she'd got to work sorting everything out as best as she could. The older girls were granted time off school while they adjusted to the news about 'Uncle Kent'. Inés wondered how this and the fear of nearly losing their mum would affect them. Chris had taken some time off too and stayed with the Cullen family, offering a protective presence in the house and a welcome distraction for the children. He started off in one of the spare rooms, but after the first night of hearing Inés' night terrors, he slept in her bed with her. She suspected it would be a long time before she was fully free of the after-effects of such a trauma.

In a strange way, though, she reflected as she shut the dishwasher door and poured a glass of filtered water, she felt as though she finally had the closure she'd needed all these years – as well as understanding why she'd needed it for so long. Perhaps, subconsciously, Inés had known something was deeply wrong, and that intuition had kept her from moving on. Or, perhaps George *had* been trying to reach her from the other side, unable to rest until his killer was brought to justice. That, of course, was Alice's take on things. Finding out that Charlie was the otherworldly intruder had done nothing to diminish her mother's belief in things that go bump in the night.

Kent was in prison, awaiting trial after having his bail refused as a danger to Inés and her family and a flight risk

– and Inés would be only too happy to give evidence. He was being tried for murder, attempted murder and fraud. She hoped he went to prison for a long time. Inés wanted justice, not only for George, but for herself and the girls who had been robbed of a husband and father, all because of his partner's jealousy and ego.

Kent had revealed himself to be a narcissist of the worst sort – and yet, he'd apparently insisted to the police officer who had arrested him that he'd always loved Inés and was only trying to protect her. Inés had so many questions, most of all, *Why?* but it would be fruitless to torment herself over what could have been. And she certainly didn't want any answers from Kent; no reason he could give would be good enough.

Finally, she could perhaps let George go.

Charlie had been temporarily placed with Inés while social services were investigating. Their involvement swiftly followed his story of why he was sneaking so often into the Cullen household and why Inés had no knowledge of his presence in her house. Bert had been ordered to keep away, but Inés suspected it wouldn't be long before there was a showdown of some kind. Bert was, after all, a proud man. She was bracing herself for it and determined to fight Charlie's corner. It broke her heart to hear how awful things had been next door for him, in that dilapidated hellhole. Inés had felt proud of her girls for stepping in to help, although she'd ordered them to apologise to poor granny for the distress they'd caused her over the past few months.

Charlie fitted in great with the girls, and Erin, Caoimhe and Alice were treating him as their personal hero, which seemed to have boosted his confidence. Inés was more than happy for him to stay; even to formally foster him if necessary and had made that clear to social services. He was part of the family, and Inés would fight tooth and nail for him to stay with them. The difference in him was so strong she could almost physically feel him flourishing. Even after only a few days away from his bully of a father, Charlie looked brighter and seemed more confident. *The hero worship was helping, no doubt,* Inés thought with a smile. After all, Charlie had saved her life.

Finished with the housework, Inés grabbed her jacket and went out to the car to pick up the girls, smiling as the warm sun hit her face. In spite of the upheaval, what with the court case and the social services case, right here and now things were okay and she felt glad to be alive. A calm settled over her as she left to collect her youngest daughters from school, just like any other day.

At the school she met the twins and then went to the reception entrance to pick up Lily, flushing when she saw Raff. She hadn't seen him since he'd tried to ask her out for coffee the previous week. That seemed like a lifetime ago. The memory came flooding back but seemed insignificant after everything that had happened. She wondered if it would be awkward. Instead, the look he gave her was filled with concern. Of course, the situation with Kent had been all over the local papers and had made it into some of the nationals. Inés didn't know for certain who'd tipped the press off, but given the preening she'd displayed when reporters showed up at the door, Inés would bet her last pound that Alice was responsible for that. Thanks to the coverage making them the talk of the village, she'd had no choice but to tell the twins about some of what had happened, but thankfully Lily was young enough to be blissfully unaware of any repercussions. Elizabeth had been round with a bottle of gin and a million questions, but thankfully, Chris had dealt with her.

'Inés, how are you?' Raff asked, the corners of his eyes creased with concern. He lowered his voice, glancing at Lily to make sure she wasn't listening, but she was too busy swapping friendship bracelets with her classmate. 'I saw the newspapers. I wanted to come and see you, but I didn't want to impose.'

'Oh, that's kind of you,' Inés said, feeling touched. She looked at the twins. 'Fiadh, Imogen, can you take Lily to the car for me while I have a chat with Mr Taylor?'

She watched as the girls skipped off, then turned back to Raff. A soft breeze ruffled his floppy fringe, and not for the first time she thought how he seemed as though he'd be more at home in a period drama than running a school.

'It has been difficult this week,' she admitted. 'There's so much going on, it's surreal in fact. Lily doesn't know about her father and I've told the twins as little as possible, but of course they're affected by the unrest, and I've had to keep them away from the papers and the news all week. We have our neighbour's son staying with us too at the moment. Family troubles. Could you ask the girls' teachers to keep an extra eye on them?'

Raff nodded. 'Of course. We have an excellent mentor as well, so if they want to talk to anyone confidentially, we can arrange that. But what about you? You look after everyone else, but who looks after you? Do you have enough support right now? You've been through a terrible ordeal.'

Inés saw the worry in his eyes and smiled softly, feeling a warmth flow through her. He seemed to care, even though they barely knew each other beyond the playground. 'Yes, my friend Chris stayed with us at the beginning of the week; he's been fantastic.'

'I'm glad,' Raff smiled. 'It certainly sounds as though you have a house full!'

'Well, with five girls, my mother and Jane, what's a few more?' Inés shrugged, laughing. It felt good to laugh. She was leaning on the brickwork to the entrance, so engrossed in their conversation she'd barely noticed the other children and their caregivers filing past. Now it was just her and Raff.

Clearly realising the same thing, Raff looked suddenly awkward, which, Inés reflected, was usual for him, at least when he was around her. He jammed his hands into the pockets of his blazer. 'I wanted to apologise for last week.'

'Last week?' Inés felt puzzled. None of what happened had been anything to do with Raff.

'Springing it on you like that about coffee. It was

inappropriate of me. And I had no idea how much you had going on.'

'Well, neither did I at that point,' Inés said, 'and I don't think it was inappropriate at all. If I hadn't had … other plans, I would have loved to have coffee with you.' As she said it, she realised it was true.

'Really?' Raff looked so genuinely pleased, his face lighting up like a schoolboy's. Inés couldn't help but smile. Raff was refreshing to be around after the disasters of her recent attempts at a love life. Perhaps Chris and her mother were right – she needed to change her taste whenever or if ever she decided to date again.

'Yes, really,' Inés said with a sad smile. 'Of course, a lot has happened since you asked. Maybe in a few months, when this is as over as it can be, we could have lunch – assuming the offer is still open, of course.'

Raff blinked quickly and the top of his cheekbones flushed. 'I'm sure it will be,' he murmured.

Inés smiled softly. 'I'd better get to the car. Have a nice weekend, Raff.'

'You too,' he murmured as she walked away. Inés crossed the playground, watching the sun dapple through the trees at the far side, and hugged her arms around herself.

Perhaps it was time for a new beginning.

The End